MW00323948

THE SOFTEST KINKSTERS COLLECTION

ALI WILLIAMS

CLAFICIONADO PRESS LTD

CONTENTS

The Softest Kinksters Collection
Published by Claficionado Press Ltd
© 2022 Ali Williams

All rights reserved.
This is a work of fiction. Names, characters, places, and incidents either are
the products of the author's imagination or are used fictitiously. Any
resemblance to actual persons, living or dead, businesses, companies, events,
or locales is entirely coincidental.

No part of this book may be reproduced or modified in any form, including
photocopying, recording, or by any information storage and retrieval system,
without express written permission from the author, except for the use of
brief quotations in a review.

Cover design © 2021 Wolfsparrow Covers

✸ Created with Vellum

ALI'S NEWSLETTER

Do you want to find out more about my books and romance lectures? Join my mailing list and be the first to find out my next releases!

AliWilliams.org/Contact

AUTHOR, EDITOR, ACADEMIC

twitter.com/claficionado
instagram.com/claficionado
tiktok.com/@claficionado

CONTENT NOTES

Holding On: PTSD, references to an off-page car crash (occurs a few years prior), anxiety, and explicit sexual content including oral, soft kink, pleading, edging and orgasm control

Hanging On: Anxiety, references to therapy, and explicit sexual content including a Domme/sub dynamic, hypnokink, impact play, flogging, oral, masturbation, cathartic crying during play

Carrying On: Anxiety, references to a previous off-page negative sexual experience, and explicit sexual content including a Dom/sub dynamic, anal play, oral, collaring and a rogue butt plug

Turning On: Anxiety, and explicit sexual content including rope play, statue kink, orgasm denial, masturbation

Hitting On: References to bad previous kinky experiences off-page (a Domme not feeling like they could safeword; and a sub having a bad experience with weaponised humiliation kink), and negotiating kink practices, including names/honorifics, a Domme/sub dynamic and petplay

Catching On: Anxiety, explicit sexual content including a Domme/sub dynamic, praise kink, oral, face-sitting, masturbation and blindfolds

Putting On: References to a previous off-page kinky encounter that did not include aftercare, (where the sub subdropped hard afterwards on her own), and explicit sexual content including a Dom/sub dynamic, praise kink, aftercare, references to off-page kink and sex

Playing On: Anxiety, explicit sexual content including a Domme/sub dynamic, praise kink, oral, puppy play, premature ejaculation, anal play and collaring

Letting On: Explicit sexual content including a Domme/sub dynamic, voyeurism, mutual masturbation, leashes, orgasm control/denial and begging.

DEDICATION

For N.
For believing in me always.

FOREWARD

EDEN BRADLEY

I've been writing—and practicing—kink for many years. I've also read quite a lot of kinky fiction. I love the complexity, the psychology of kink. Why do we do these things we do? How does it help us explore the darkest corners of ourselves? How does it heal us? Because it can. It has. And it continues to do so, for me and for many, many others.

I love a story that really dives in deep, explores these aspects of the human mind and body. This is what fascinates me, whether we're talking about an especially great book or a real-life experience. In fiction, what compels me is when the author's true and profound love of language shines through. It's the beauty of language that makes me need to read, and when done well, causes that need to blossom until I must read more. In those lovely moments when the beauty of the words drives and inspires in a way that makes me swoon, light-headed from the sheer beauty of the prose, I am joyful, overflowing. Beautiful language makes me yearn—for the words themselves, for the characters to find whatever they're looking for, whatever they need, because the language itself has become almost another character, a mood, a tone. The words can express something in me I wasn't able to verbalize before. The beauty of language never fails to astonish me, to bring me joy, to make me dreamy, to make me yearn in a way that nearly hurts. But I like it. No, I love it.

This is what Ali Williams's writing does for me. To me. Because reading her words is an intensely evocative experience that touches me on so many levels. Because her writing does exactly what writing—particularly erotic stories, romantic stories—should do. It touches. It inspires. It dreams for us.

She's also completely unafraid to delve into those topics others may not be brave enough to approach. In her stories she discusses parts of the human psyche and experience we too often feel the need to keep hidden, and that we struggle with. She brings these things out into the light, allows us as the reader to witness a journey in which these aspects of her characters—and so often of ourselves—can be honored and processed and nurtured in a way that not only makes us believe in the healing powers of love, but makes us feel less alone. She talks about pain. She talks about anxiety. She talks about loss, particularly loss of self (and haven't we all been there?). And as we read, we respond on such a deep, visceral level because these characters, their pain, are us. They're ours. And it's an epiphany of sorts.

Her work is also redemptive, and not only for her characters at the culmination of the story, but also, somehow, for us. Her character arcs are so well described, so well and lovingly explored, so gorgeously illustrated that one cannot walk away from one of her books without feeling as if we've learned something. She opens up a universe of emotion and sensation, and I can't help but be humbled by her talent and her courage.

But make no mistake, even within the profound depth of

her storytelling is a wonderful good time! She blends kink with emotion in way that's pure perfection. She will titillate and delight. She'll set your imagination—and your libido—on fire. And at times she'll make you smile, and even laugh. What a divine combination!

Ali herself is so like her characters. Lovely and self-doubting, utterly sweet and oozing sensuality (and she'll blush like mad reading these words, but they had to be said!). But that's part of her magic, and the magic of her storytelling.

Come with me: Let's get lost in her stories. You won't regret a single moment.

Eden Bradley
New York Times & USA Today Bestselling Author

THE SOFTEST KINKSTERS COLLECTION

HOLDING ON

*S*he'd gotten lightheaded the first time that they'd kissed.

They'd been at her favourite bookshop in town and he'd been talking about listening to War of the Worlds on repeat, half singing little snippets of it to her, and all she could think about was the fact that she wanted him to kiss her. That for all their attraction to each other, for all his swagger and his ability to make her laugh, that it was this version of him that she wanted to kiss the most; sweet, a little self-deprecating, and ever so slightly geeky. And she'd found herself stepping up close, laughing at what he said, and then looking at him. There'd been a moment when his words died on his lips and he looked at her back, and that moment? That was the moment when she realised that this would be a Kiss.

And it was. He could kiss. He could *really* kiss. It had been gentle and sweet, and then as she deepened it, their lips scalding against each other's, he'd pulled her flush against his body and she found herself being thoroughly kissed in a manner that made her heart beat that little bit faster and her glasses fog up in a way they hadn't in years. If his hand hadn't snaked around her waist, anchoring her, she wasn't entirely sure that her knees wouldn't have given way. Then they'd come up for air, eyes averted, suddenly shy, with a slightly awkward laugh and a glance round to see if anyone else in the shop had seen them, when all she'd wanted to do was to grab the lapels of his shirt and pull him back towards her, to lean up against the bookshelves and kiss and kiss until they were dizzy with desire and she could feel him again, hard against her thigh.

Each time they'd met, it had been exactly like that. Spending lazy afternoons in pubs, singing their hearts out in karaoke bars, dancing at spontaneous gigs on the beach. They'd walk and talk for hours, eating up days and moments, as if time didn't exist. He'd tease her in a way that made her blush until he apologised in a half laughing voice that said that he wasn't all that sorry really, that he liked seeing her shy and laughing and flustered. And then eventually that look would creep back in. She'd catch his eye and there it was again. That need to be kissed.

She wasn't quite sure why it was that he affected her like this.

No. That was a lie.

There was the fact that he was funny, and a little more cool than she knew what to do with, and just the right amount of nerdy. And he was interested in what she had to say and her opinions; wanted to know her. Wanted her to take up space in his life. There was a comfort between the two of them that made her want to bare herself to him, to let her vulnerabilities and softness unfurl petal by petal until he held her delicate fragility in his hands. And when he kissed her there was laughter and desire intermingling in his eyes as he captured each gasp that she breathed out with his lips. Fingers dancing along the underside of her knee – the most innocuous of movements, but one that drove her wild – and then the feel of his breath along her neck as he bent to kiss along her jawline. They were the sweetest of moments. Ones that made her head spin with dreams of kisses pressed against her lips on Saturday afternoons on the couch in front of the tv.

And now she was here, at his flat. By his front door. The first date at his place.

She paused momentarily, not wanting to lift her hand to knock into the possibility of something going wrong. Up until here, up until now, anything could happen. But the moment that she stepped through that door, anything would. She'd end up spilling something on the carpet, or coughing at a really inopportune moment, or even embarrassing herself by shrieking at a particularly jumpy point in the film they'd planned to watch, and finish it off by falling off the sofa. None of those things appealed, and whilst she was outside the flat, none of them were actually happening.

It was, she decided, the Schrödinger's cat of romantic possibilities.

She'd probably have waited outside for far longer than was entirely necessary if he hadn't opened the door, all ruffled blond hair and easy smiles. And then she felt all kinds of comfortable, all kinds of relaxed, reassured that he wouldn't laugh at her too much if she really did fall off the sofa.

Stepping into the apartment, he leant down to kiss her cheek, lips caressing her skin in a movement that made her sigh involuntarily, and then flush as his blue eyes met hers, amused. Delighted by that giveaway sound.

"Hey."

"Hey."

Words that would usually flow, unbidden, to her lips froze upon her tongue as she found herself grinning at him, unable to keep a smile from floating across her face. It felt like there was a warm glow inside her, one that heated her up from the inside out, and as his hand glanced against hers as she handed him her coat, she couldn't help but smile a more secret smile to herself.

It had never been like this.

Never.

The mere touch of his hand made her want more. Need more of the comfort between them that promised sweetness shot with fun and laughter. It made her think of afternoons sat on the beach, eating fish and chips and dodging aggressive seagulls. It made her think of running through summer storms for shelter, dripping wet and yet still laughing. And it made her think of being safe; of being able to just stop and cry in his arms.

She found herself slipping her hand into his, their fingers intertwining in a dance that ended when he tugged her towards him in one swift movement, bending his head to brush her lips with his.

His mouth was gentle but firm against hers. A sweet kiss. One that said how much he wanted to have her here, with him, in this moment of their making. And she kissed him gently back, her hand curling up to caress his cheek as she felt herself unwind. The remnants of tension, of the anxiety that had hounded her before she'd arrived, just melting away against the warmth of their touch.

Then one quick kiss dropped upon her forehead, where it sat, branding her skin with him, as she took her shoes off and they went into the living room.

It was a relief to realise that she wasn't going to have to explain her need to shuck cushions off couches before she could sit down, but she still stood, slightly awkward, until he raised an eyebrow in question. And then she sat next to him, bolt upright. All that nervousness edging its way back into the corners of her mind. She could sense him leaning back, finding that spot on his sofa that was his and she felt just so damn lost. Sat frozen like she didn't want to curl right up against him, to lie her hand against his chest and feel the thud of his heart beneath her fingertips.

It had been too long.

Too long since she'd sat with someone like this – shared space on a couch together – and she wasn't entirely certain that she knew how to do it. How did you go from sitting upright to that casual lean back, where thighs and arms kissed against each other? She didn't even realise that she was fidgeting, her fingers dancing a tarantella against her knees until his hands reached out to partner them in the dance.

Looking up, those blue blue eyes caught hers and she smiled shyly, loosing one hand to run it through her hair, the action allowing her to break eye contact for a moment and recentre herself. Allow a little equilibrium back into the moment.

She breathed in. Once. Twice. And then met his gaze head on this time. She watched as he stretched out one arm along the back of the sofa and she found herself curling inwards against him, the fragility of her trust fluttering against his like a butterfly's wings. His arm curved around her, and she raised her hand to rest against his chest, just like she'd wanted to do, and breathed out. This was okay. It was okay. They were okay.

With his free hand, he grabbed the remote and then they settled down to watch a film with less gore than she'd feared but a hell of a lot of jumpy moments. After one particularly startling scene, she buried her face in his shoulder, half-hiccupping with laughter that was not at all in any way covering the fact that she'd squealed far too loudly for her own liking and had almost thrown the glass of water that he'd brought her at the screen.

It was at that point, however, that he seemed to give up all pretence of watching the film. Moments of stolen glances put aside for a single finger under her chin, dancing eyes meeting her own embarrassed ones, and this time she was the one who kissed him. Who leaned up into his space and captured those laughing lips. And she'd captured his softness as well as his laughter. There'd been a split second where she felt as if she'd fall, Alice-style, into the kiss. Falling down down down until she landed in a space where her heart took up an echoey beat that reverberated around them both, where she became too big or too small to ever really fit back into the real world again. Fuck White Rabbits, this kiss was her pathway into Wonderland.

And then it had shifted, his hands cupping her face with an urgency that seared her skin. Branded her with fire. Her hands mirrored his until they ran through his hair.

One kiss. Two. Three.

It was seamless, the way that they deepened the kiss. Both of them caught up in the intensity of the closeness, of the emotion of it. They paused for a moment, taking shallow breaths that ghosted lips that were mere millimetres apart and she realised that she was halfway across him in a weird up-on-her-knees and splayed-across-his-front way, without actually straddling him. She shifted awkwardly, almost toppling over until he caught her and righted her.

"I'm a little clumsy," she explained, brushing her hair from her face and looking away.

He leaned in and kissed her gently. "You can be clumsy with me any day."

The gurgle of laughter that pealed from her made him smile, and he tugged her further onto his lap. "Wouldn't want you to fall again."

She grinned and shifted 'til she was comfortably astride him, trying not to let out a gasp of delight as she felt him hard against the seam of her jeans. "I wouldn't want to fall off this."

There was a momentary pause where they both seemed torn between more intense making out and just full on laughter and before she added, "God I'm bad at this."

"Not at all." He pulled her closer as she put her arms around his neck. "You. Are. Perfect." Each word punctuated with another kiss until she leaned in and stole all his sentences. There was a slight desperation in their kisses this time, a need to get as close to each other as possible, the freedom of having a private space emboldening them both. His hand skimmed the edge where her shirt met the top of her jeans, and she found herself hitching it up, before pausing and whispering in his ear so he didn't see her blush, "Can you...?"

"Can I what?" Each word buffeted against her neck and she gasped once, and then again as he traced the curve up to her jawline with his mouth. "Tell me, what do you want me to do?"

The words burst from her in a rush. "I need your hands against my skin. Please. If you don't mind−"

But before she could even finish her request his hands were cool against her skin, teasing, coaxing little gasps and moans from her as they ran up her side and back. A questioning glance as her top ensnared his hand, and then she reached down to hoist the shirt up and over her head, laughing as it got her glasses got in the way.

When she'd finally untangled herself enough to look back at him, her breath caught in her throat. The look in his eyes, darkened irises that drank in every single inch of her curves, made her blush and want to both cover up and take more off.

"What?" she asked, the questioning sounding almost defensive.

"You're just so..." That pause seemed like a lifetime. "So beautiful."

"Yeah yeah, flatterer." But she felt warm inside, even if she didn't know how to tell him how much those simple words meant. That he wanted her, all of her, with her big arse and her big tits and her clumsy attempts at stripping.

He laughed at – no, with – her, and she leant in to kiss his right cheek. He swallowed and she ran her hands down his front. "Your shirt. I mean, can I take it off?"

"Of course."

One swift motion and it was up and over his head, and as it floated down to the floor beside them, he sat up, shifting so that they were face to face, chest to chest, the sudden skin contact warm. Almost as warm as her core as she felt his cock rock up against her. She wondered whether her longing was painted in broad strokes across her face, whether he could tell that she just wanted to lose herself in the warmth of his touch until everything blurred together in the slick heat of their longing for one another.

His hand was tentative against her breast, a searching gaze looking for an acquiescence that he found in her eyes, before his fingers traced the edge of the bra cup, dipping in and grazing against her nipple in a way that made her cry out. Previously, she'd always felt incredibly self-conscious about how sensitive she was, the fact that she couldn't control or moderate her reactions, but this time was different. This time she found herself relishing in being able to show him exactly how much she liked this. How much pleasure his fingers were bringing her. Because fuck if he didn't have magic fingers that coaxed all manner of sounds from her throat, his pupils darkening when she reacted.

And she savoured each moan and gasp he drew from her. Let that tight control over herself go until she was loose-limbed beneath his touch.

She slipped a hand down between them to feel the hard outline of his cock through his jeans and grinned at the curse he muttered against her neck. It was affecting them both then; this all-consuming passion had hit him just as hard as it had her. There was something very satisfying in that, in the knowledge that this wanting, this need, was mutual. That it wasn't just her losing her mind over something as simple as a make-out session on a couch.

Another kiss, more fumbling, and then, as they both came up gasping for air, a slowing down. Not an awkwardness as such, but more a wave of shyness that crashed over them both in a sudden about turn.

They laughed softly, averting their gazes before sneaking looks at the other under lowered lashes.

"I had planned on feeding you before getting into your bra."

She snorted. "Well, it's never too late for food."

She wasn't sure quite whether this was a rejection, or just a postponement, but when they got up to move to the kitchen, he slipped his arms around her, hugging her close, before ushering them through to the other room.

This was intimacy of another kind, casual laughter together as they heated the food he'd prepared – tasting the sauce for the pasta, grating cheese and grabbing cutlery from drawers. It spoke of an easy comfort between them, and made her realise how much this meant to her. Cooking together, for each other, seemed such a key tenet of affection, proof of something more than people merely passing through each other's lives.

When they ate at the breakfast bar, she sat, legs curled up beneath her, and they talked as they ate, spooning warmth with every bite. The smear of sauce across his mouth would have been easy to wipe off, if it wasn't for the fact that he turned to press sauced lips against the inside of her wrist, infusing that simple action with a heat that took her breath away. Red to match the lipstick she'd left on his neck earlier. She'd muttered something about mess and thrown her paper napkin at him, but she'd been secretly delighted, had want to revel in the mess with him.

Even washing up together had been fun. She'd washed and he'd dried because, as she pointed out, she had absolutely no idea where anything went, but it had been an excuse to flick soap suds at him and then get chased around the kitchen in mock indignation before she let him catch her. Back to the door, arms braced either side of her until she smiled invitingly up at him and he moved in to kiss her again, his mouth stealing kisses she wanted to give him forever.

Dates like this didn't happen every day. She'd had enough experience to know that. To know that this comfort and ease with each other, as if they'd been together all their lives, wasn't the usual. To be able to flit from eating to kissing to laughing to comfortable silence in a space of moments.

When she'd gone to leave, each kiss of the afternoon a shadowy imprint on her skin, she'd almost told him how happy she was. How euphoric the afternoon had made her feel. But before she could, he'd pulled her in close and whispered how lovely she was against her lips, and how smart and funny and it was all she could do to not mount him right there by the shoe rack.

Instead, she'd kissed him again. Lingering this time. Slow and sweet and sensual and full of all the words that they'd left unspoken. Full of the promises that she wished she could make, the blossoming trust that she had in this new thing between them.

But when she closed the front door behind her, and looked out at the seafront, she realised with a crashing sense of foreboding that it was raining.

Normal rain wasn't a problem. A light shower, even a heavy shower, wouldn't be bad. She could drive in those just fine, but this? She swallowed once, twice, as the waves crashed against the shore, the sound of pebbles being dragged back over each other again and again echoing *that* sound and– She shook her head.

No. She'd worked so damn hard to move past this; the months of therapy, of developing coping strategies that were meant to help her in moments just like this one. She reached out for the coping statements that she'd worked on as a grounding tool with her counsellor and murmured them to herself over and over. "I can handle this. This will pass. The rain won't last forever."

But it wasn't until she was stood there, hand frozen on her car door handle, hair plastered to her back as the rain lashed against her skin and every rumble of thunder made her shiver, that she realised that no. She couldn't. She really couldn't drive in this.

It seemed unbelievably unfair. It wasn't even as if she'd been the one driving the first time around. No physical scars. Everyone fully recovered. But that didn't prevent a wave of dizziness that overwhelmed her senses and threatened to cast her back into the unending loop of that night, her breathing falling back into that pattern of panic that she hated so. In and out so fast that she could feel her control unravelling.

Stop.

A long breath in. Held, then loosed in a barely contained rush.

She took a second, slower, jagged breath and realised that there was salt water mingling with the rain on her face. Tears betraying her.

A moment to make a decision. She could get in the car and sit and rock until the storm was done, to relive the sounds of that night until she became a sobbing mess; she could walk to a nearby pub, and to hole herself up in the bathroom until one of her friends could come get her; she could even give herself a ten minute break in the corner shop across the road and then attempt the drive once more.

Or perhaps... No. The thought of him seeing her like this, broken and bedraggled, made her want to throw up almost as much as getting in that car did. But he *was* sweet and kind, and if she really wanted this relationship to go anywhere, then she had to be honest with him, had to show him this. Or at least she could dash the tears from her eyes and ask him if she could wait out the storm at his.

She shifted from one foot to another, and made a split decision.

This time, no Schrödinger's cat of romantic possibilities whilst waiting on his doorstep. Just fear and anxiety and more nervousness than she'd felt in aeons.

But he opened the door, took one look at her, and gathered her inside. No questions. No "what's happened?!" Just bundling her into the bathroom with huge fluffy towels and a hoodie that would dwarf even her curves, and a "what hot drink would you like?" question that she hiccupped out an answer to. Then the door closed behind him with a quiet shuck and she was left, just her and the bedraggled figure in the bathroom mirror, mascara painting their cheeks.

A step forward and she forced herself to meet her own gaze, her own reflection and then, slowly, she peeled back the damp clothes that clung to her, each layer a step further and further away from the feeling of pounding rain drenching her, drowning her in memories and pain and–

A knock at the door.

"Hey." Not quite a question, not quite a statement.

"I'm okay." Words gasped out as she felt panic threaten to engulf her. She looked down at clothes pooled around her feet, and a vague sense of bemusement at the starkness of her skin against improbably cheery underwear. Then jagged breaths as she grabbed the hoodie and pulled it up over her head, wet hair damp against the soft material, the hem falling to her knees.

But he didn't say anything, didn't reply, just waited until she pushed the door open and stood there, shivering in the onslaught of her emotions. It was one thing to be at the start of a new relationship, to be open with your feelings, to show that delicate vulnerability that caused a frisson of excitement. This was not that.

This was more than anxiety and catastrophising, this was drowning in memories and emotion and being a wreck of a person. This was not who she was. Not who she wanted to be. Not who she wanted him to see.

So she didn't look at him. Didn't look up into his face, didn't see the pity or the concern in his eyes, didn't even take a step out of the bathroom. She was stuck. Knee deep in quicksand that was rising fast. Opened her mouth and then closed it. Because how on earth could you explain being in this kind of state after a perfectly nice – a perfectly *wonderful* – date?

She almost jerked backwards as a hand brushed against her cheek, and it paused there for a moment. Waiting. Checking. And then it lowered the hood that covered her hair and replaced it with a fluffy towel.

There was something incredibly soothing about having her hair towel dried by him. She lent forwards unconsciously and found herself so close. His body heat warming her as slow movements, delicate deliberate movements, towel in hand against hair, helped ground her.

The quicksand subsided.

She took a shaky breath. And then another. And another. Small jittery breaths until she was slowly but surely breathing again. A little jagged still, sure, but in a regular rhythm that didn't threaten to throw her off-kilter.

The towel moved away and he replaced the hood back up over her hair, and she found herself grateful for his understanding that, right now, the last thing she wanted to show him was her tear-stained face.

She pulled her hands up inside the sleeves, and used the corners to wipe her eyes, her cheeks, head still down, until they dropped, mascara-stained to her sides.

"I've got your hot drink in the living room, if you want to come sit down?"

A silent nod, and she followed him quietly, small little steps, shadowing his. Her hand reached out instinctively, and she felt him look behind to where she held onto the back of his shirt. Her sudden loosening of her hand and a step back placated with a smile and a nod of approval, before she held on again. And then they were in the living room, and he was curling around her. Arms enveloping, warming, protecting. The aforementioned drink in a mug so big that she cupped it in her hands like a bowl. Small sips. Small breaths. Her world slowly righting itself.

She'd never really found comfort in silence before. Bustling sounds and chatter kept her busy, kept her thoughts distracted, kept her from overthinking and reliving again and again, but this was comfortable. That comfortable silence that she'd read about in books. She put the mug carefully on the coffee table, leaned back, snuggling in, and sighed as his hand tentatively touched her hair. Gentle strokes that calmed her and made her want to lose herself in his quiet, in his gentle touch.

She didn't realise that she'd fallen asleep until she awoke suddenly, jerking upwards, disorientated and confused.

"What–? Where–?" and then as realisation hit, apologies tumbling over each other in a waterfall of sorries, the words barely able to keep up with her racing thoughts, a jumble of panicky self-recrimination. *You idiot. He must think that you're pathetic, you're–*

"It's okay." His hand beneath her chin, lifting it 'til she met blue depths. "It's fine." They weren't just words; he really didn't mind.

Then he grinned suddenly, adding teasingly, "You make cute little snuffly snores when you sleep."

She reddened, hiding her face in his shoulder in embarrassment, even whilst she was grateful for his lightening of the mood. "Oh hush up." He hugged her close and she found the courage to whisper, "Is it still raining?"

It was later than she'd hoped, but it was also still apparently storming, and the look on her face must have caused him some consternation because he said abruptly, "You can stay here tonight, if you like. I'm sure the storm will be gone by morning."

She looked at him sideways, and he shook his head, "You know I didn't mean it like that, but I'd rather you stayed than left if it's going to upset you."

A slow nod. "That would be...good. I'm sorry about all this, it's just..."

"You don't have to explain, no apologies. It's fine, I promise. Now, I'm thinking leftover pasta and Netflix. There's an animated space series that I think you're going to love."

It was, she realised as he went to set everything up, his way of caring. Little tactile displays of affection that made him move with purpose. He wanted her to lean on him, to trust him.

"I was in an accident."

The bustle stopped and he came and sat down next to her, even as she couldn't look at him, couldn't do anything other than fiddle with the hem of the hoodie and blurt out words that made her want to curl up and hide. "There was a storm.

An accident. And we're all fine now. No longer term. Injuries but still. I. I. I don't like driving in storms. Not that it was me who was driving in the first place and I guess that means that I should be fine with driving in storms now and I can't and I just couldn't sit in the car and wait it out because when it hits the windshield like that over and over and over I just–"

His arms again. Round her again. Comforting her again. "Shh. It's okay, petal. You don't have to talk about it; you're here with me, and I'll keep you safe."

For some reason, after that, she felt less awkward, a little more like herself again. Comfortable enough to snort with laughter when a sentient spaceship repeatedly denied a dorky character a chocolate chip cookie, and comfortable enough to flick pasta sauce at him when he tickled her to make her laugh some more. And she'd never been quite so grateful for streaming services' enabling of binge-watching; they worked their way through more than a few episodes, curled up on the sofa together, until her head kept dropping and she was fighting to keep her eyes open.

"Time for bed?"

She nodded, all of a sudden, feeling a little reticent, and he smiled gently at her concern, his hands cupping her face for a kiss. "I'll need to grab spare bedding so that I can bunk down on the sofa here, but after that, my bedroom's all yours. And I have a huge duvet that you can cocoon yourself in if you need to."

There was a pang of sadness as she realised that actually, she really wouldn't mind him curled up round her, under said duvet, but he was right. This was probably for the best.

So instead she followed him down the corridor to where a large king-sized bed waited for her. One so large that she thought she could get lost in its depths. She perched on the edge of the bed as he got the linen he needed for his own repose, as well as a spare towel for her, pointing out where she could charge her phone and where the switch for the lamp on the bedside table was. Some laughter. A long look that had her flushing, and then a gentle kiss that was as intense as it was tender. As he went to move away, she found her body following him, led by her lips back to his for another.

"Good night, petal." He whispered the words and she whispered "Good night" back, and sat there, teetering on the edge of calling him back as he left the room and closed the door quietly behind him.

Settling beneath the covers, the bed seemed unnaturally large. Too large to settle in the middle, with each side legions away. Instead she set up on the starboard, glasses folded on the bedside table and light on for some reading before she slept. She might have been sleepy earlier, but now? Now she was far too awake to sleep. Every inch of her longed for his arms, for his touch, for his kisses, and the only way she was going to be able to distract herself, was to read a little before bed. Lose herself in a different world until she was too tired to focus on the words on her phone screen.

It might have helped if she hadn't been reading a paranormal romance, all turbulent shifters and hot sex, but even the world building wasn't enough to divert her attention from where she could still feel his lips on hers, the shadow of his touch on her breasts. She toyed with the idea of touching herself, of casting her ebook to one side and letting that tight control unfurl from her as she lost herself in thoughts of him. But she was in his bed, and that seemed a little unfair.

She could go to him.

She could *ask* him to come and sleep with her, even if actual sleep was all that they did.

Her face flushed at the idea of it. The idea of going and asking for what she wanted. What she needed. It seemed unlikely, she realised, that he'd find that abrasive. He'd liked it earlier when she'd asked him oh so politely if he could touch her. And even if he said no, she didn't think that it would be awkward.

Momentarily emboldened, she slipped out of bed and hurried to the door before she could lose her nerve and change her mind. But as she approached the door to the living room, she paused, suddenly shy.

One step. Two. And then she peeped round the doorframe.

He was sat on the sofa, blankets tossed casually on the coffee table, and he was watching a sitcom on the television.

"Ummm...?"

His head turned and she found herself dropping her head, and playing with the sleeves of the hoodie again. "You okay, petal?"

"I...I was wondering if you wanted to... I mean, it's a big bed and I..."

He stood and walked over to her, one finger under her chin, raising it 'til she could meet his eyes. "What is it that you need?"

"You." She blurted out the word and would have turned her head away sharply to hide if his eyes hadn't sparkled. Blue eyes, shot with a splash of gold, that were kind and happy and hungry. *Oh*, she realised, *he wants me*.

She'd technically known that already, especially if their make-out session earlier was anything to go by, but to realise it now, when her body was humming with need and he was close, oh so very close to her, well. It was certainly something.

He moved his finger so that his hand cupped her cheek, and then the nape of her neck. "Tell me again. What do you need? *Who* do you need?"

"You. Please." Her words were more resolute, more unwavering than she'd ever known them, and she felt a jolt of pleasure when his eyes darkened at that second word. At her pleading.

And then his mouth was on hers, hot and demanding, walking her backwards until she could feel the wall flush behind her, and at some point their hands brushed against each other, tugging fervently at the hoodie that slid over her head until she stood, clad in nothing but her underwear, his eyes caressing every inch of her.

"I want you too, petal. I want you writhing beneath my hands, my mouth, and I want you to cum apart on my cock. Would you like that?"

She squeaked in reply, desire momentarily stealing her voice, and nodded eagerly, desperate to have him put his words into action.

He laughed then, delighted, this deep warm sound that felt like a stroke against her clit and she leaned towards him for another kiss. "Please?" In this moment, she thought that she'd do anything to feel him for real against the throbbing of her clit, his fingers replacing the caress of his voice, as she let go for him. Let it all go.

Then he was taking her hand and pulling her back into his bedroom, to that bed. Drawing her along, drawing her towards him, until he gestured to the bed, adding with warmth in his voice, "Sit down, I can't have you falling over."

Despite that, she almost fell over in her hurry to sit down anyway, her peal of laughter at the irony ringing out echoed by him. And that was good. Laughter was sexy, even if tripping over her own feet wasn't.

"I'm sitting down."

"I want to make you feel so so good, but you need to trust me. Do you trust me?" As he spoke, he started to unbutton his shirt. She watched his hands' deft, swift movements, undoing button by button – as if there were any other way to unbutton a shirt.

She nodded, wide-eyed, as her lips parted and she leaned upwards for a kiss.

"Wait a moment."

She stopped. Waited for him.

"How will you tell me if it's too much?"

"Too much?" This was all too much already, too much waiting, too much tension, too much not enough-ness.

"Oh petal, I intend to make you come until you lose your mind, til you're begging me for a breather. So how will you tell me if it's too much? If you need a break, or you need me to stop? Because otherwise I'll just keep going and going."

She took a jagged breath, suddenly desperate for air. The thought of coming for him again and again had her pussy clenching and her clit throbbing. He chuckled at the look on her face. "Oh, you like the sound of that?" His belt was tugged through belt loops, then dropped to the floor, before his hands paused at the top button of his jeans. "Well then? How will you tell me?"

Her right hand tapped three times on the bed. Tapping out. Because she had a feeling that if he was going to make her come as much as he said he would, she might need a sign that didn't involve speaking.

"Oh I like that, petal, tapping out like the fiercely strong fighter that you are. Okay then. That's your sign. Now, move back for me."

His jeans were gone and she had a glimpse of a hard length straining against his boxers before she scrambled up the bed. He followed her and then, with confident hands that fumbled a little with the complexity of the clasp at her back, he undid her bra, sliding it down her arms and cursing softly as the fullness of her breasts came into view.

"They're not," she found herself stammering, "gravity defying," but he put aside her self-consciousness with a single kiss, reaching behind her to adjust the pillows, that small movement belying affection and tenderness far beyond the lust in his eyes.

"I don't need gravity defying. I need you," and then slowly, gently, he pushed her back until she was lying before him. Laid out for him, lace hiding soft curls, and breasts aching for his mouth. With tantalising slowness, he lowered his lips to one nipple and sucked, pinching the other with his fingers and she moaned out loud without meaning to. He looked up and met her eyes, lifting his head briefly so that each word he spoke teased the wet puckered peak he'd just had in his mouth. "I love it when you moan. I want to know each and every time I make you feel good, so you be as loud as you want for me."

She fought the urge to look away, to hide her shyness from him, but instead met his eyes and nodded slowly. And he kept her gaze as he lowered his mouth back down and made her moan again. Each lick and suck and gentle bite had a direct line to her clit, she realised. That he had her squirming beneath him just like he said he would, and when one hand danced along the lace gusset of her underwear, she realised she was wet for him too.

Well. Wet might be slightly underselling it. She was sodden, the material drenched through, and as he stroked her gently through it she closed her eyes and arched up against his fingers.

"Aren't we greedy?"

Her eyes flew open and she looked at him in such alarm that his hand moved swiftly to cup her cheek. "No no, petal, that's not a bad thing. I love how needy you are for me, how desperate."

"Oh okay, that's good." Her hammering heartbeat settled back into its echo of the throb between her legs. "I don't want you to think that I'm too much."

He kissed her slowly and deeply. "You are perfect. My

good girl. And if I make you greedy for me, then I'm very lucky, aren't I?"

"Yes, yes you are." Her mischievous laugh was cut short by a gasp that he elicited with a stroke. Just. *There.* "Oh, please. *Please.*"

Hands urged her hips up and soft fabric dragged down her legs and tossed aside. "Please? Please what?" Each word accompanied by a kiss on her inner thighs, getting closer and closer, and she moaned in frustration.

"Please, please kiss me."

"Here?" He partnered the single word with a kiss just above where she felt her need thrum through her clit.

"Noooooooo."

His chuckle had his breath dancing across her pussy and she arched up, trying desperately to reach his mouth. "Come on now, use your words. Where would you like me to kiss you?"

"Please please *please* kiss my pussy."

"Good girl," and with that his tongue licked all the way up her pussy, ending with a swirl around the sensitive nub at the top.

The noise she made then was somewhere between a moan, a gasp and a sigh of relief, and it seemed to galvanise him further. Each lick against her clit had her breathing quicker and quicker, the intensity of his touch making her spiral higher and higher until she found herself teetering at the very edge of something, reaching out for a release before he pulled back, dropping a single kiss on her glistening pussy.

"Wha...what?"

"Not quite yet, sweetheart."

"But..." She was speechless, so utterly desperate to come and yet...

His hands skated across her skin, tracing patterns across

her thighs, her stomach, her breasts, until they lay against her cheeks with his face close to hers. "If it's too much for you, that's okay, I promise I won't be disappointed. All you have to do is give me the sign."

She met his gaze, her body thrumming with need and the reassurance she saw there strengthened her resolve. "I think...I think I can take some more."

This time, his lips stayed against hers, teasing and demanding, as fingers danced against her clit, in a rhythmic pattern that made her feel like she were a bass guitar he was playing. An instrument beneath his fingers, ready to sing.

He stroked her once more to a peak, and once more pulled her back from it.

It was almost too much, to be so mindlessly brought to the point of release and then left there, left dripping and aching and yearning for that moment when he'd take her, waterfalling down into bliss. And yet, she felt so free. No catastrophising thoughts crowding her brain, no panic pushing out peace, but this almost serene neediness. Wanting. She was at her most vulnerable, completely open to him, and yet she felt the strongest she'd ever been. She was strength and power and desire all in one, and as he slipped his fingers inside her, the come hither movement stroking against her g-spot, she thought she'd shatter.

"Are you ready for me, petal?"

"*Please.*"

She followed his glance to the bedside table and nodded before he opened a drawer and grabbed a condom. And then his eyes were on hers as he entered her oh so very slowly.

She felt so full, so tight, so damn ready and as he began to thrust she found herself pleading again and again and again. The sweetness in his smile almost took her breath away and then his hand slipping between them to rub at her clit did exactly just that, stealing her breath and her words and pushing her higher and higher until "Come for me sweetheart."

And she did.

She rode each wave that swept over her, gasping and writhing and coming beneath him, around his cock, just as he said she would, and as the peak seemed like it was coming to an end, he pushed her into another crescendo.

"I think you've got some more for me."

He had her, a delicate, trembling thing, breaking in his arms over and over. Each wave taking her further and further away from anything other than this. This moment. She'd never before been so in the present, been so utterly in the here and now, with nothing else cutting in.

From somewhere far away, she heard him swear and then he was leaning in so close that she could have counted his eyelashes if she'd been so inclined. Not that she was in any fit state to do anything other than moan and plead in a never-ending cycle that had him kissing her and then coming with a murmur of affection that made her melt.

It took her some time to come down from the heady heights to which he'd taken her, and when she did, she found she was wrapped up in his arms, her trembling hands clinging to him as he kissed her cheek and stroked her hair.

"Oh. That was..." she trailed off uncertainly.

"It really was."

"Thank you."

He pulled her in tighter. "You are the sweetest thing; thank you indeed. Thank *you*."

"No." That wasn't it. The sex had been amazing, and she was fairly certain that she was still experiencing aftershocks, but she wasn't thanking him for that. "Thank you for looking after me, during whatever fireworks display that just was, to holding me after. And earlier. During the rain."

He looked serious as he met her eyes. "That's something

you never need to thank me for, that's part of it. If you need me to, I'll hold you. Whether it's through tears or sighs or the most adorably cuddly aftercare. You trusted me with your vulnerability, with yourself, and I would never take that for granted."

She felt a smile roll across her face until she was grinning so uncontrollably that she hid her face against his chest and felt his rumble of laughter.

"And you holding on to me right now, petal? It does me the world of good. That's my aftercare right there."

She nodded, still curled up against him, untucking her head until she could meet those blue eyes with her own unwavering gaze, "Then I shan't let go."

"Exactly. Never let go, petal mine."

HANGING ON

*T*he waiting was almost unbearable.

It'd been so long since they'd sat down together, had some food, kinked it up, that she couldn't help but feel a little anxious. A little nervy.

Her leg bounced. Up down up down, her heel tapping the hardwood floor of their front room.

It would be fine, she knew that too. She loved her wife and her wife loved her and yes, they had to deal with being apart for far longer than either of them wanted on the regular, but it didn't change their connection when they were together.

And yet this last month had been awful. Really bad. She'd been overwhelmed by work and she'd pushed through until she couldn't push any more. She'd had to take days for her mental health because she'd started shutting down, zoning out in meetings, struggling to get up in the morning, abandoning all pretence at attempting housework.

Her anxiety didn't get this bad very often, but when it did, she felt so overwhelmed that there was little she could do to banish it. Those small little coping strategies that she'd developed with her therapist worked best; choosing to do things that brought her joy, or at least that didn't stress her out more. She just wanted to curl up under a soft blanket on the sofa and watch crappy tv shows until she passed out. Wanted to shrink the world down to that one sofa, so she didn't have to get up, didn't have to move, could just try and shut out the thoughts that clustered her brain. And so she did. Sofa breaks with plenty of pillows and blankets and water.

Her wife had seen it in her face the moment that they'd video called. Had used *that* voice and made her promise that after their call she'd run a bath, soak in it, bring herself a little release. And then had promised her a date night upon her return.

"When I get back, I'll take it all away for you."

And that had quietened the thoughts for a little while, or at least it had whilst she was in the bath, submerging her shoulders in the water and reaching down to stroke herself to orgasm. A brief relief. A brief break from the constant carousel of anxieties that circled her brain, dragging her round and round until she couldn't focus. Water eased that. Made her think about floating, and coming helped too.

It was never as satisfying though, coming on her own, but her wife was right. She needed something. Going too long without did something to her brain chemistry and she got all desperate, and not in a fun, kinky way. The kind of desperate that resulted in the tightening of her chest and needles at the back of her eyes, pricking until tears forced their way out. That made her fix her hair over and over, hands fidgeting, fluttering about her until she wanted to scream from the frustration of not being able to let go. That needed cuddles and hair strokes to calm her down, and need to hear that it was okay. That it would be okay.

Long leisurely strokes. Keeping her promise. Coming for her love.

It was a moment that she could hold on to, a foreshadowing of the relief that would come when her wife got home. They'd talked about this, about how being on her own for so long whilst her wife travelled with work wasn't ideal, but she usually coped much better than this. Spoke to her therapist, sought out the support she needed, only her therapist was on holiday and there were only so many times she could call the local mental healthline before it felt too much. Before everything felt too much.

But she needed a break. She needed a break from everything in her head, and she'd been promised it and it was all that was keeping her going right now. It tore her in two, almost. Torn between wanting to see her wife, to hold her and kiss her and talk to her about her month; and wanting her wife to be Ma'am, to take on that persona where she became Her. Ma'am always brought relief.

She peeked out of the window, running a finger across the light chain of her collar as the rumble of a car sounded in the street outside. And then there her wife was, as tall as she was short, striding towards the door, a suitcase rattling along behind her.

The sound of the key in the door.

A pause to try and get her nerves under control. Failing. Heading into the hallway anyway and then that smile that lit up her life, lighting up the room. Her wife's blonde hair feathering across her face as her wife closed the door, and then falling around her as she was pulled close and thoroughly kissed.

It was almost instantaneous, that moment of relief. Even just walking through the door, her wife had made her feel better, feel loved, and being held – head tucked tight beneath her wife's chin, face turned in against the swell of her wife's breasts – was the best feeling of all.

Well.

Maybe not quite the best.

A single finger lifted her face up until she met soft grey eyes, like she'd done thousands of times before.

"Welcome home," she whispered, fighting the pricking of tears behind her eyes. No tears were going to fall now. She would not allow it. This was not sad, this was happy, but her wife knew her too well, and lent down, dropping the softest kiss on her forehead.

"Thank you sweet one." And then she was pulled back into those arms, a hand cupping the back of her head, anchoring her, and she finally let silent tears fall.

After, her wife went upstairs to unpack whilst she finished dinner, almost floating on air as she hurried from stove to countertop, pan to microwave, and then balancing plates as she brought everything through to the table.

A candle lit in the centre of the table, surrounded by food, music on in the background – just as if this were a private restaurant for two – and her wife walking into the room and glowing when she saw the spread.

Cooking like this, for someone else, was as personal as sex for her. Literally giving them something that would keep them alive, and hopefully taste pretty damn good, all at once. And this meal radiated care, from the time it had taken to prepare, to the very food that she'd chosen. There couldn't be a clearer declaration of her love than if she'd shouted it from their attic window.

"Oh you wonder, this looks delicious!"

Traitorous blushes stained her cheeks as she pulled out a chair for her wife, before sitting opposite. Wraps with spiced filling, apple salsa and that hot Thai sweet chilli sauce her wife loved so much, made for good eating. And they talked as they always did. With each moment that passed, she could feel the tension in her shoulders lessen a little, her load lightened by her love's mere presence.

But at the back of her mind there was that voice, talking, catastrophising. *You're asking too much of her. After a day of travelling, all she wants to do is eat and sleep and expecting anything else is too much. Such demands are outrageous. Too much. You're too much.* She hadn't even realised that she'd gone quiet until the woman across the table from her stopped talking and said softly, her words not judgemental or tired, but calm and patient. "Are you panicking?"

"A little."

"Well, we can't have that now, can we."

She watched, caught between panic and relief, as her wife slipped into the seat next to hers and took her hands. "I promise that I am looking forward to our scene as much as you are, sweet one. It's what's kept me going all day, and I don't want you to worry about it. I suggested this, I want this. So breathe. Please."

So she did.

Small, quiet breaths in and out until she started up their conversation with a joke about travelling woes, and listened happily to all that her wife had been up to.

When it came to dessert – ice cream with all the trimmings – she'd put it in a big bowl so they could share, the two of them still sat next to each other, spoons nudging as their thighs rested against each other.

Even salted caramel on her tongue, her favourite flavour, wasn't enough to make taste her dominant sense. No, every fibre of her being was concentrated on touch. On the touch of their kissing thighs. On the touch of her wife's foot running up and down the inside of her calf. On the touch of breath against her ear every time the woman next to her turned to say something.

Her breath hitched, audibly, and her wife grinned wickedly before nipping at her ear, and then her spoon was clattering against the side of the bowl and she was kissing those lips that had called to her all throughout their meal. Hot, passionate kisses that silenced those careening thoughts until they were so far away they were barely on her consciousness.

"Please," she whispered, words drawn from her lips before she even knew that she spoke them. "Please, do what you want."

"I will."

The promise galvanised her, before her wife picked up the abandoned spoon, topped it with ice cream and offered it to her. "One more spoonful, and then I get to do what I want."

She couldn't eat it fast enough, and then was up out of her chair, and looking expectantly at the other woman's bemused face. "Upstairs?"

"That's right. Upstairs. Get changed. Sit on our bed, and wait for me."

Heading upstairs made her heady. Wanton. Ready. Hands trembling with excitement, fluttering by her side as she turned to her dresser. What to wear what to wear what to wear.

She wanted something that would make her wife smile, both in that delighted aren't-you-pretty way and in that I-can't-wait-to-ravish-you way, and so instead she turned to the drawer under her bed, and picked out her powder blue babydoll, allowing its soft sheer laciness to slip through her fingers once, twice, before placing it on the bed and discarding the clothes she wore as quickly as she could.

There was something almost ritualistic about getting ready like this. The slide of clothes against her skin as she pulled them up and over, down and off. Folded, put in the laundry pile, like she was putting away that her, and putting on this her. The quietness that came with the babydoll; tying the ribbon round her neck, behind her collar, and there, she was settling into being that her. That shift in mindset that made her a little more breathless, a little less composed. Checking herself in the mirror, struck by the peekaboo of pussy beneath the flirty hem and the dusky pink of her nipples, teasing through the material. Strokes of a brush through her hair, a kiss of lipstick and she was done.

When she sat on the bed, she noticed for the first time that her wife had switched the covers before she'd come down to eat. She'd picked out the super soft white comforter that always made her feel like she was sitting on a cloud, floating way above the earth, and her nipples tightened in anticipation. Floaty play was her favourite kind of play, cloudspace the best kind of headspace.

Because her head rarely shut up. Just crowds of thoughts tussling with each other, fighting to be heard. Books helped, as did sex, but being completely and utterly in the present, with nothing else to distract her? For that there was cloudspace.

She bounced up, and sat back, letting the babydoll settle around her, skirting the tops of her thighs, and showing just the right amount of leg.

Now she got to wait again. Got to wait on her wife to enter the bedroom and be Ma'am, just for her.

She fidgeted, the sheer blue the perfect distraction from her excitement. Because she *was* excited; she was almost trembling with it. If this had been another kind of day, if they'd been doing a different kind of scene, she might have edged a little, might have run her fingers across her wet slit and flicked at her clit, but it wasn't, and she'd been told to wait.

Waiting was torture.

A good kind of torture, but torture nonetheless. When she was this her, she was a good girl and did as she was told, but it still itched: the longing to touch herself; to call out for her wife; to do something, *anything* rather than just sit here and wait for what would come next.

Being a good girl was hard sometimes, when her head wouldn't quiet and her fingers danced across her lap, but being a good girl made Her happy, and she'd do anything to make Ma'am happy.

"Such obedience." The mellow tone of that voice had her looking up and over to the doorway. Her wife had that leather jacket on, the one that made her go all melty inside and want to do anything for Her. It shouted Ma'am and she knew that she wanted to feel it against her skin, cold through the lacy blue that she'd donned.

And then she noticed.

There was nothing under the leather jacket.

She melted, drinking in the curve of Her breasts and the soft swell of Her belly before feasting her eyes on the pussy that she hoped she'd be allowed to feast on later. "Look at you, all tucked away on a cloud," and now it was *that* voice. The one that helped all of her fears drift away. "Tell me angel, what happens if you feel like you're going to fall off your cloud?"

"I say yellow Ma'am."

"And if your cloud disappears altogether?"

"Red Ma'am."

That smile of approval warmed her down to her very toes, and she wriggled on the comforter.

"And any time you say those words it'll bring you right back here to me."

Even as she felt herself relax, she felt the command become concrete in her mind, real and true. A golden line back any time she wanted it. "Thank you Ma'am."

"My angel."

At that, she beamed and wriggled again. Being Hers was wonderful. The only thing better was being...

"My *floaty angel.*"

She wasn't sure she'd ever quite be able to explain what it felt like to have her 'floaty angel' trigger used to someone who didn't do hypnokink. She'd tried, once or twice, to other kinksters and they hadn't quite gotten it, thinking that it was some kind of elaborate roleplay, but it wasn't. Not really.

She felt her head droop a little, and she was vaguely aware of Her coming close, and helping her lie back against the pillows.

Floating was fun.

Floating was...perfect.

"How's that cloud feel, angel?"

"Soft..." the words fell out of her mouth without her bidding, and she relaxed into that feeling. She just *was* right now. If Ma'am asked her a question, she'd answer it straight-away. No thinking, no pesky thoughts, just straight truth. And it did feel soft. As her eyes drifted close, she practically felt wisps of cloud beneath her fingertips.

"And you're my soft floaty angel too."

She let Her voice drift over her, guiding her.

"But those thoughts you have are too heavy to be sitting here with you on that cloud, so we're going to take them away for a bit. How does that sound angel?"

She giggled then, all then tension in her body dissipating, because she knew that Ma'am was right. Heavy thoughts really did have no place on a floaty little cloud like this. "Yes please Ma'am," she said, "Please make them go away."

A hand settled in her hair, and she knew that it was Hers, and she felt herself drift some more.

"Well, you know what happens when I stroke your hair angel."

"Yes Ma'am," there was a little brightness in her sleepy voice for a moment, "You stroke my thoughts away."

"That's right angel, each stroke sweeps a thought out of your head-"

"-and you blow it away."

There was affectionate laughter in Her voice at that. "Yes, and I blow it away. And why is that?"

"Cos lil angels don't need heavy thoughts weighing them down."

"Exactly."

And then it started.

Each time Her hand moved across her hair, she felt a lingering thought caught and removed. In her mind's eye, each thought almost looked like a dandelion seed, the dark kernel at the bottom containing a multitude of anxieties that got blown away by Her.

As each thought left her head, she felt lighter and lighter until she reached out to hold Her hand.

"Are you still on the cloud angel?"

She nodded, a little dazed, "I'm not falling off, I just-" she paused, searching for words that were beginning to elude her, "I don't want to float away."

She felt a kiss against her forehead then, and then Her hand wrapped around her wrist. "You won't float away angel, I won't let you."

That was all the reassurance she needed before she let herself drift into that lovely headspace. 'Floaty angel' was her very own shortcut into subspace and it helped her *feel*. And she could feel everything: each individual finger that anchored her wrist; the soft soft cloud beneath her arse; the gauzy material of the babydoll against nipples that ached to be touched. Even the damp curls between her legs. She felt it all.

She whimpered then. "Please," she whispered.

"Please what angel?"

"I...I...I don't know!" And she didn't. Her thoughts were

gone and she was completely free of anything and everything except Her, but it wasn't quite enough. Not yet. What she wanted, what she *needed*, was just beyond her grasp.

"Of course you don't angel, but that's what I'm here for. Come, open your eyes for me sweet one."

She opened her eyes slowly, blinking at the sudden light, and caught sight of the pale blue flogger in Her hand. "Oh."

"Now then angel, you told me that you've had a very stressful month."

"Yes Ma'am," she whispered, eyes still following the slow swing of the flogger's tails back and forth, back and forth.

"Have you cried at all?"

Her eyes widened and she slowly shook her head. Crying was relief, was release, and it wasn't something she could easily indulge in. Angels got to indulge in whatever Ma'am said though.

"Would you like to?"

Vigorous nodding.

"Well okay then, arse up!"

She scrambled onto all fours, and grabbed a pillow to rest her face against. Waiting. Again. This time, with her head light and airy from 'floaty angel', the waiting was less torturous. More meditative, as if she were centring herself.

As if.

No, she was *definitely* centring herself.

"I'm not going to ask you to count them off angel, because I want you to float into tears and that won't happen if you're counting, but I do want you to tell me what your words are."

"Red. Yellow. Green." Traffic lights that were so ingrained into her, that even in the deepest trance she could still recall them.

"Good angel."

The tresses of the flogger were draped gently over her back and ran slowly down until they fell about her arse.

"My angel."

And then it began.

Flogging worked better for her than a caning; too sharp a sting and it brought her right up out of subspace. Same reason why Ma'am had slipped a pillow over her feet, because pain there made her safe out so fast her head would be spinning for at least an hour. But the slow rhythmic thud of the flogger sent her hurtling deeper into that space where her thoughts were as blank and as white as the cloud she'd floated on.

She breathed slowly, taking in larger breaths when she took a particularly heavy thud, and smaller ones when she needed to breathe through.

The rhythm was slow at first, giving her time to adjust before Ma'am picked up pace and strength until all she could do was just let go and give over to the sensations that thudded into her over and over again.

She hissed as a particularly hard crack caught the edge of her clit, and then moaned. The pain always gave way to pleasure, waves of thuds rolling over her much like the waves of an orgasm, and she felt herself dripping even as the pain receptors in her brain started to short out.

This was it. She knew it. When everything became too much. When having nothing in her head but this moment and these emotions and these *feelings* rolled over into...

She started to sob, curling her fists up in the softness of the comforter and allowing herself to simply let go. Shaking. Trembling. Her whole body wracked with the physicality of finally letting everything go.

She heard the flogger drop beside her on the bed, and then Ma'am was behind her, enveloping her with Her warmth and Her body, Her small breasts pressed up against her back. She cried harder. It was easy to cry when Ma'am had her, when she was able to let go of everything and just let it all out. It was why she sometimes cried when she came; the release of both so close, so similar, so much. And right now this was what she needed, to be enveloped by Her completely. To let Her hold her as she broke in just the right way.

Ma'am moved onto Her side, and pulled her in close, tucking her into Her body, and began stroking up her back her sobs lessened. It was both aftercare and also a sign that it was time to come back from that space she'd been lost in. Time to let her breathing settle, and return to the world of the non-tranced.

It took a while for the sobs to recede, for her breathing to calm, to feel more her again. This time when she opened her eyes, she met her wife's gaze and smiled. "Thank you."

"Thank you?" There was laughter in the other woman's voice, "Thank *you* angel, for trusting me so. How are you feeling?" She shivered as her wife's hand skimmed the skin of a rather sore arse.

"I'm good." Then, as that hand dipped lower and ran across the slick wet entrance to her pussy, she added, "More than good."

"I'm glad to hear it." She didn't know how her wife could sound so calm and collected whilst casually fingering her, and yet here they were. "Perhaps we could push from more than good into great? And then maybe you'd like to show me just how grateful you are for your cloudspace time…"

Arching up as her wife slipped inside, curling her finger in a come hither kind of action, and running her thumb across her clit, she gasped out. "Yes please, I would like that very very much."

The throaty laugh that answered her was cut short as she leaned forward and grabbed the lapel of the leather jacket, dragging her wife towards her for a kiss. She wanted it like this, her arse still tingling from the flogging, her head still slightly spacy from the trance, and her lips meeting her wife's as she gasped and moaned and clenched around those fingers that teased her so.

Her wife hit the g-spot, of course. She always did. And damn it felt good, sent her keening and pleading and begging all at once against the other woman's mouth until she increased the friction on her clit and she came apart beneath her hands.

It wasn't that she was seeing stars, but rather that she'd become them; been sent flying up into space to shatter into a million tiny twinkling stars, stippling the sky with her pleasure. Not just relief, but release.

As she came back down to Earth, slowly drawing herself back together, she looked at her wife and smiled. "My turn."

She pulled her wife up, that leather jacket earning its keep, and spun them so she was on top, smiling down at where those blonde tresses decorated the pillow. Making her way down her wife's body was always fun, but when they played so hard, she always liked to be effusive in her thanks.

Licking round her left breast, she murmured her pleasure as the nipple pebbled under her tongue, and when she drew it into her mouth, she was gratified to note the moan that accompanied it. She'd missed that sound. In fact, she'd missed so many things about her wife. The way that her skin goosebumped as her mouth left her nipple. The curve of her wife's body as she arched up against her. And this feeling that burrowed itself beneath her skin, that she was doing this, that she was making her wife feel cherished and loved and oh so very very good.

She played there for a while, letting her hand tweak and tease the other whilst her tongue and mouth were busy lathing and sucking, until her wife's hips began jerking upwards impatiently. She took pity on her then, sliding a hand down between them even as she kissed her way up her wife's collarbone to that sensitive spot on her neck.

She bit down at the same time that she slid her fingers into her wife's hot warmth and was pleased to note how she bucked under her, that tight pussy tightening around her fingers just as her wife gasped and cried out every time her neck was touched.

And then, leaving the air cool against the leather and her neck, she slipped down her wife's body so that her mouth could join her fingers at that point of elixir.

She loved cunnilingus.

There was something so immediate, so *intimate* about being at that very centre, about caressing her lover's clit and slit with her tongue. About working her mouth in concert with her fingers over and over until she achieved her ultimate objective. Orgasm.

Rushing it, though, was not her style. She liked to tease a little, the way that her wife teased her as her Ma'am. To draw out each peak onto an edge that she prolonged before finally tipping her over into pleasure. And she started on this now, varying the rhythm of her movements and the intensity of her licking so that her wife couldn't quite get there. It wasn't topping from the bottom; it was knowing her wife and knowing what she needed, just as Ma'am had done for her. Drawing it out made it that much more delicious when her wife did come, and she felt that pleasure as keenly as she felt her own. And so starting and stopping it was.

Her wife gave a delicious gurgle of laughter, and then sat up, leaning back on her arms and glaring amusedly down at her. "No fair."

Lifting her mouth from where it had been quite happily sipping on nectar, she kept sliding her fingers in and out as she raised an eyebrow. "No fair? I don't know what you could possibly mean!"

"Argh!" There wasn't any real annoyance in the exclamation, and she knew it for sure when two hands wove themselves into her hair and tugged her forward, back to work.

That felt really good, the hands in her hair, a little like the fingers around her wrist made her feel anchored. It made that connection between them stronger, more intense. And she moved her fingers, her tongue, her mouth with more and more urgency until she could feel them tighten in her hair and then she moved off. Stopped altogether.

There was a little petulance in her wife's urging hands this time, and she held off until she heard her say "Come on, *please*," before she started up again.

She could have spent all eternity here, lapping at the nectar of this goddess of hers. Eternity losing herself in the taste and smell of this pussy before her, but her wife would probably have had something to say about that. Something along the lines of "Damn it, I need to come!"

She was too caught up in her wife's taste to catch the exact phrasing but the meaning was clear. And so when she heard cursing above her once more, she sped up again, wanting, *needing*, to tip her wife over into undulating waves of pleasure that would be as satisfying as if the orgasm had been her own.

There.

She felt that hot pussy start to spasm around her fingers and murmured her approval as the other woman's back arced up off the bed, and then the legs either side of her face were trembling and moans were filling the air.

Losing herself in her wife's pleasure like this was addictive, made her continue until that moan became a single note of delight that would pulse through her brain. Doing this, serving like this, always made her feel subby but – perhaps because of the play they'd already done, or perhaps because of the month she'd had – she found herself hurtling back down into that trancelike cloudspace without warning.

It wasn't until a hand urged her face up that she realised she was still licking. Her eyes focused on the face above her, and then unfocused again, her vision blurring, and when she felt her wife's hand slide through her hair and down to her jawline, she moaned and clenched her thighs together, trying to get that oh so tantalising friction that would bring her relief.

The hand held her chin in a grip that was as kind as it was unyielding and brought her up until she flicked a peek upwards. In that moment everything blurred, wife and Ma'am, bed and cloud, up and down.

"Oh." The word was whispered. "You really have struggled this month, haven't you angel?"

It wasn't a question that required an answer, that was clear even to her fuzzy head.

"It's okay, you can spend a little more time in cloudspace with me if you like."

She found herself nodding urgently, pleadingly, as the modulation of her wife's voice changed until it was Her again.

"Come lie back for me angel."

Her body moved of its own volition, limbs heavy as she lay back and felt herself sink into the softness of a cloud once more. A knee nudged her legs open and she giggled nervously as cool air caressed her pussy.

"I'm so proud of you," Ma'am continued. "To let go for me like that, to be pretty and pliable and so good at pleasing me. But I need you to let go a little further angel. I need you to let go of everything and trust that I have got you."

She murmured an acquiescence and let everything drop; legs so loose that they fell open, jaw relaxing until her lips parted softly, eyes closing and shutting harsh light out. And all the while, Her voice, caressing.

"How do you feel sweet one?"

"Yours."

"Exactly. *My* angel. And do you know what I want for my angel?"

Even shaking her head was slow now, as if everything in the universe had slowed down so that it could focus on this one tiny moment, in the place, in this space.

"I want my angel to feel good, sweet one. Are you safe on your cloud?"

Now to nod. Slowly her head moved up and then down. "Yes Ma'am-" words blurred into each other as she spoke them, "-I'm on my cloud."

"And if you're going to fall off, or it disappears...?"

"Yellow and red Ma'am."

Somewhere, at the back of her mind, something clicked into place. That safety lock that she needed, reenforced, double checked. Normally Ma'am wouldn't check as much as this, but normally she wouldn't have slipped back into cloud-space on her own.

"Good angel. And good angels need to feel good. Can you make yourself feel good for me sweet one?"

The words that Ma'am had spoken caught in her head and she found herself whispering them over and over, breathing them out until they became a part of each outbreath. "I'm a good angel. I'm a good angel."

Mantra fixed in place, she found herself moving her hands, one to her clit, the other to her nipple. Pinching and playing. She let her hand revel in her wetness, fingers slipping and sliding across her entrance, and then in and out and then up to rub at her nub that made her ache.

"Such a good angel."

Ma'am was stroking her hair now, each stroke sending

her more lightheaded, until all she could do was murmur "I'm a good angel," over and over and over, fingers dancing across her tits, her slit, her clit as if they were being puppeted by someone else.

Perhaps they were.

Perhaps all she was, was an empty little puppet, being held up by strings. Ma'am coaxing mewls of pleasure out of her, making her sigh and moan and feel good. And she wanted to feel good. Ma'am said that good angels needed to feel good and she was a good angel. She needed to feel good. She needed to feel good for Her.

The moan that interrupted her mantra startled her into a giggle.

"Good angel. Good angels are happy and good angels feel good."

And then she was moaning and giggling and giggling and moaning in a never-ending loop that made her clit thrum with need.

Giggling made her happy, and being happy made her feel good, and then that made her feel *really* good, and she floated more and more, each giggle making her pussy clench and her nipples tighten until she was so so floaty that Ma'am caught her wrist to make sure that she didn't float away.

"Does that feel good angel?"

"Yes Ma'am thank you Ma'am yes Ma'am thank you Ma'am." Words were now waterfalling, chaotic and continuous, as she babbled whatever came into her head. And whatever came into her head was what Ma'am had put there so it was a mix of Ma'ams and thanks yous and I'm a good angels again and again and again until she lost control over her words completely and they melded together into one long cry as her orgasms burst over her.

Waves crashed again and again and again and she was

shaking. Trembling. Coming apart. Falling apart. Anything and nothing all at once.

They lay there for a long time, no words, no debrief, just lying in each other's arms. She wasn't sure that she'd be able to speak even if she tried.

All she wanted to was to hide herself from the world, to curl up against her wife and breathe until everything came together again. Until she could face coming back up again.

It took a while this time round, coming back up. A quick count up to normal wouldn't work here, they both knew that. Instead, her wife whispered sweet nothings in her ear, praising her, telling her what a good job she'd done, saying how proud she was of her for letting go completely like that. The praise coaxing her back. Coaxing her up.

Slowly – and it was slowly – she lifted her head up out of treacle and blinked a few times. Everything seemed a lot in that moment, everything except the woman who held her in her arms.

"Hey," she whispered.

"Hey yourself. You back?"

"I think so." She reached out with her mind, searching for the little thoughts that interrupted her daily schedule. They were there, she could sense that, but she could also sense that they'd been put away for a while. On a shelf just beyond her reach. "Thank you, I know it's a lot-"

"No," her wife was firm. "It's not a lot. It's a delight, having you give over everything to me like that. You trust me with your body, your heart, your mind, and it is the greatest gift anyone could ever give me. I will never take it for granted, and," she added with a sudden grin, "having you so desperately pleading and babbling like that, hanging on my every word? Well, it's just so damn hot."

She blushed and ducked her face. "I wouldn't do it for just anyone."

"I know. I know sweet one."

It was something she'd only ever done with her wife, given up complete control of everything like that – well, almost complete control, traffic lights always applied – and it was something that they explored together. Sometimes as straight play, where emptying her head became a game so sexualised that it almost became a challenge to see who'd come the most, but sometimes, like this. A scene which was more about relief, about a break from the anxieties in her head that rarely shut up.

And though her wife took on responsibilities in the scene, they were the same responsibilities Ma'am always took. She knew that, because they'd talked about it. Hypnokink wasn't the solution for her anxiety – she had a therapist for that – but sometimes it helped her open a valve and let the pressure escape.

And she was so fucking lucky that she had someone so wonderful to help her with the valve when it got stuck.

At some point they would move so they could snuggle under the comforter. At some point they would probably get up and brush their teeth and do all the normal things they'd usually do before going to bed. But not now. Now was just the two of them, breathing in this space that was theirs. Together.

CARRYING ON

*F*aceplanting on a bed was never ideal.

Even more so when said faceplanting followed an attempted striptease.

She lay there – face down on her pillow, jeans tangled up around her ankles – and wondered exactly how it had gone quite so wrong.

It had all started out rather innocuously. The sexy look over her shoulder, the wiggling of her bum (accompanied by a most satisfying smack from her boyfriend), and the long kiss? That had all gone according to plan. Even the discarding of her top and bra had gone without a hitch. Each button had undone smoothly, and the hooks of her bra had come free more easily than they usually did.

But then she got to her jeans.

She blamed him, sitting there all sexy, his eyes eating her up, caressing each inch of skin that was revealed to him. It was all his fault that she'd gotten distracted.

First the button on the top of her jeans had got stuck. Then the zip. And then her shimmy had turned into a wriggle, then into a half-pirouette as she spun round, whilst trying to get those damn skinny jeans off, and voila! Face-planted on the bed.

A bed that was now shaking a little.

Turning her head, she met his inevitable grin with a rolling of her eyes and a laugh of her own.

"You're such a delicate flower," he said and she stuck her tongue out at him.

That probably wasn't a great idea. Bratting never ended well, or ended very well indeed, depending on the sub's perspective.

He raised an eyebrow and then leaned over her, catching her legs as she tried to kick off those damned jeans. "Oh no, Buttercup, I think I like you with your jeans around your ankles."

Each hand encircled an ankle until she stopped wriggling and let herself relax into his touch.

"Good girl."

And then those hands were skimming across her skin in that thoroughly tantalising way that she loved and hated in equal measure – teasing, caressing, driving her to distraction – until they caught on the lace of her knickers. She felt him run his thumb across the edge of them, caressing the skin of her arse, tickling her and making her wriggle.

"Wriggly girl." A short smarting slap against her arse, and she almost begged him to take her. "What should I do with you then?"

There was a pause and then he kissed her shoulder, "Go on sweetness, what should I do with you?"

"Whatever you like?" There was a playfulness in her response, and he chuckled and kissed her shoulder again, hooking his fingers under the sides of her knickers and drag-ging them down until they reached her knees. No further. Restraints without restraints. "Oh…I…Sir…"

"Oh? I? Sir? None of those are suggestions, Buttercup."

She swallowed, suddenly nervous. She wasn't quite sure what to say, or how to be in this headspace and tell him what he should do. She didn't want to do that, she wanted – needed – him to tell her what they were going to do. She-

"Shhhhh." Suddenly his fingers were entangled in her hair, tightening around loose curls until he pulled her head up off the pillow. "Look at me."

She did, albeit cautiously.

"I've got you. It's okay. I can ask your opinion, but I have the final say Buttercup, so silence those thoughts and tell me what I should do."

She didn't say anything, instead reaching for the drawer beside the bed, and picking out the bottle of lube that was in there.

That was easier than saying it, which they both knew, and so she wasn't surprised when he nudged her gently towards actually vocalising it. "Come on, Buttercup," his mouth was right up against her ear and she could feel his breath batting against her, "that's not telling me. Tell me."

She swallowed once, twice and then buried her face in the pillow again before muttering, "My arse, I want to…please play with my arse, Sir."

His soft laughter was kind and it made her want to hide away a little bit less. Not much less, but just enough that she no longer had to hide herself away completely.

"Good girl. I'm so proud of you for telling me. And I also think that I should play with your arse." He smoothed his hand down her back, "Would you like spanks first?"

Oh, so this was going to be a vocalising session. They'd had to work on that when they'd first started playing together – saying out loud what she wanted was difficult after the experience with her ex – but kink play meant consent, and they'd worked on it together until she felt she could say what she liked, and occasionally what she wanted.

It also meant that they had nonverbal cues for when it all got a little bit too much for her to handle, and she appreciated that more than he would ever know. To know that if she slipped into a space where she couldn't answer, or where things were too much, that all she had to do was snap her fingers, just once, and he'd stop.

She'd even tested it out a few times, to make sure that he wasn't just saying it when he said that he'd respect her safeing out, and it had always come with cuddles and a large bottle of water to drink.

"Spanks first please, Sir." She was pleased with that. Once she'd have avoided the word spanks altogether, but now she was choosing it; complicit in her pleasure.

He said nothing, but she could feel how pleased he was with her. She always could. There was something about him, about the two of them together, that resonated with her. Made her feel safe in knowing his emotions.

"I'd like you to count off for me, Buttercup; can you do that?"

"Yes, Sir."

"Good girl. Twenty spanks coming up."

She smiled into her pillow. He was cute; soft Doms were the best. Funny and sweet and warm. She needed that warmth always.

The first spank wiped the smile from her face and she hissed at the impact. "One. Thank you, Sir."

She could practically hear the smile in his voice. "You're welcome, Buttercup."

The next landed on the other cheek and she bit out the count and her thanks.

It wasn't fast, no shower of spanks that would overwhelm her too quickly. He needed her all warmed up, so was taking his sweet time. Pauses between each one. A caress here. A tickle there. And as she sunk into subspace she felt it all: the soft pillow against her face, muffling each cry and whimper that escaped; the lace of her lingerie, caught around her knees, catching her; even the weight of her own arms by her sides, almost merging into the bed. And she felt the strikes most of all; the smart they left behind and the way it grounded her. Kept her in the here and now. With him.

When he stopped for longer than the other pauses she realised that they'd already reached twenty. Her arse stung and her face was wet with tears. She wanted more. She wanted to ask for more, but then he was stroking her clit, and confirming how desperately wet she was for him, she forgot anything else she'd ever wanted altogether.

She wanted him. His pleasure. His delight in her. His pride.

"Thank you, Sir."

"You're very welcome, sweetness."

And then his hands were gone, reaching – she guessed – for the bottle on the bedside table, and she knew she was right when she felt it cold against her arse. His finger, slick with lube, rubbing around her hole, and then into the tightness.

Deep breaths. Slow, deep breaths.

She liked anal play, loved the way it made her feel so full, so tight, so delicate. Loved the way he held her and looked at her when she pushed herself for him. When she tried for him.

One finger, and then two, and he was kissing her shoulder and whispering sweet nothings in her ear that she couldn't quite grasp because all she could think was how much this was. So much.

"Buttercup?"

"Yes?" Her answering question was a ghost and she realised that he'd hardly heard it. "Yes Sir?"

"Where are you at?"

"Oh, green Sir. I'm green. This is good." And then his free hand was back in her hair, pulling her up so he could kiss her cheek.

"I'm proud of you, sweetness."

His words almost made her glow. That's what she needed. That reassurance. And possibly- "More?"

"What was that?" His teasing tone made her giggle shyly.

"More please, Sir."

He could have asked her more what, but she was thankful when he laughed. He knew what she meant by more; they both did. So when he slowly withdrew his fingers – wiping them on the towel beside the bed, there for just such a purpose – she tried her best to relax into the waiting. To focus on the here and now. The sound of another drawer opening and closing. The sound of the bottle lid opening.

Then the touch of a cool flared plug against her arse.

Her princess plug. Not the silicone one, which had a little give in it, but the glass one that they'd only used a handful of times, with the adorable heart-shaper jewel at its base.

"Come on, Buttercup, spread for me."

She reached behind and pulled her cheeks apart, face flaming against the pillow, and as he pressed the glass against her, she struggled to breathe, tensing up and making it all that much harder.

"Yellow."

The pressure subsided immediately, and he moved it away. "Good girl for telling me. Do you want to stop?"

She shook her head, face still pressed against the pillow.

"You've tensed up?"

She nodded, and he kissed her shoulder again, almost branding her with his affection.

"Well, we can't have that now, can we? Let me know which way your lights go, okay sweetness?"

"Yes Sir." Her voice was small this time, but determined.

She wanted to relax, but the more she thought about it, the harder it became.

He slipped his hand between her thighs. Dipping into the pool of wetness at the entrance to her pussy and then slid it up her lips to her clit. Just like pressing a button, her shoulders started to loosen. Okay. This was okay.

Maybe a little better than okay.

Definitely better than okay.

And then there was a moment when he rested his hand against the small of her back, palm flat, and she was able to breathe again. Relaxing against his hand, relaxing with him. Completely and utterly calm; all tension dissipated. "Green."

"Green it is."

A moment as he applied a little more lube, and then that pressure against her as he slowly worked the plug inside of her, little by little, until she could feel the large flare of the base against her skin.

It hit her then, that overwhelming feeling of fullness that always came with a plug, and the satisfaction straight after.

It wasn't the satisfaction that she got after an orgasm, or even the satisfaction that she got when he was hilt deep in her pussy; this was a deep-rooted satisfaction in the fact that she had pushed herself to take more for him. She knew he'd be proud of her, but in that moment, when she was breathing hard and trying to concentrate on centring herself once more, she didn't care so much about his praise as much as her own.

This was her choice.

She wanted this, had asked for it, and had been granted it.

She deserved this.

She was worthy of this moment.

"Where are you at sweetness?"

"Green." This time, her voice didn't sound timid at all, but rather boldly open. She turned her head to look back, over her shoulder, and met his eyes straight on for the first time since she'd faceplanted on the bed. "Will you fuck me please, Sir?"

The tenderness with which he looked at her made her heart sing. "My god you're amazing. Of course, Buttercup, of course I'll fuck you."

Slipping one arm beneath her, he lifted so that she could scramble onto her hands and knees, kicking off the jeans that were still caught on her feet. But the knickers? Those he ripped off her, first the sodden gusset, and the lace at the side. "I'll buy you a replacement, I promise," he murmured as he moved behind her, "but right now I don't want anything keeping you from me."

The sound of his zipper – which he appeared to have no problems with, thank goodness – was brusque in the quiet between them, and after shedding his jeans, he pulled her hips up flush against him, so she could feel his hard cock, jutted up against her.

She rocked backwards, desperate for him now, wanting that overwhelming fullness to envelop her completely. And he obliged.

Slowly, so slowly that it was almost torturous, he slid inside her, inch by agonising inch. She tried to move backwards, but a sharp slap to her arse told her no, and his hands kept her in place. No, he was in charge, and she loved him for it.

As he drove home, she gasped and then he began to move, the slightest gyration sending shivers up her spine and making her clench around him and around the plug. It was a lot, yes, but it felt so fucking good too.

And she'd been so fucking good, so she got to have this moment, with him, and it was everything.

"Fuck, Buttercup," he said, the gravelly need in his voice making her moan. "You feel amazing, sweetness."

That was when she got lost.

Nothing but the smack of skin against skin, and her lost so deep in subspace that she went to that whiteout space. Just blankness. And him. Grounding her. Anchoring her.

Again and again and again, she moved backwards and forwards, making noises that she wouldn't have recognised, yearning for that something just out of reach.

Faster now, building and building, hot tears racing down her cheeks in quiet need, until she was almost, just almost-

"Fuck!" He jerked backwards and fell to the side of her on the bed. "Cramp cramp cramp!"

It took her a moment or two to realise what he was saying, to pull herself back from that almost orgasm and roll on to her own back to look at him.

He was rolling around, jackhammering his legs back and forth, trying to alleviate the pain and she couldn't help it. She giggled.

He looked at her, and for a moment she thought that maybe she'd done sumat wrong, but then he started laughing too, and then they were both laughing, proper belly laughs that shook their whole bodies and made breathing hard in a completely different kind of way.

When they could finally breathe again, he cupped her face and kissed her. "You are the sweetest sweetness there ever could be. I'm so sorry."

"No," she pressed a kiss into the palm of his hand. "No sorries. It's okay, I'll just have to distract you from the cramp a different way."

He looked at her in question, but she knew what she wanted, and moved down to take his cock in her mouth. It had softened somewhat, understandably, but she liked the feel of a hardening cock in her mouth. Gave her a sense of accomplishment.

Rather than talk with her mouth full, she popped her head up and grinned at him. "Oh, you don't mind if I...?"

"No no," he gestured at his cock. "Please, be my guest."

It took her to a different kind of subspace, cock sucking, and she suspected that there were as many different subspaces as there were sex acts. This was fun. Almost service sub-like, making sure to give as much pleasure as possible. She always got a little determined to take it a little deeper in her throat than the previous time, to make him swear or make a noise, or say something that he hadn't before.

Joyful.

That was what it was.

Perhaps that was a little strange, but she enjoyed sucking his cock. Liked how it made her feel, how it made him feel. Velvet on her tongue. She hadn't always enjoyed it this way, but he was so encouraging, peppering his exclamations with "good girls" and "my precious Buttercup" and the touch of his hand against her hair made her want to keen up against him and nuzzle her head in his hand. Only she didn't, she controlled herself because she had a job to do and that job was getting him as hard as she possibly could.

Bobbing up and down, delicately playing with his head, choking herself until she could feel his legs tighten up around her... It gave her a sense of achievement.

And all the while, there was the plug in her arse, insistent and hard, never letting up with that pressure inside of her.

She slipped a hand down between her legs to rub her clit and he brushed his hand from her hair to her cheek.

"Enjoying yourself there, sweetness?"

She mmmmed back her answer, and he laughed, sliding his fingers through her hair until her curls were tight in his grip and he started moving her more insistently up and down his cock.

"Good girl. My wet and needy Buttercup, taking my cock so damn well. Come here." And then he was pulling her up so she was astride him, and he rocked up to brush his cock against her clit and she almost cried.

"Wow sweetness, you're very needy, aren't you? Do you want my cock?"

"Yes, Sir, yes please." She leaned forward so that she could feel his cock nudge against the entrance to her pussy and she almost took every inch of him in a single movement, but caught his eye and stopped, frozen for a moment.

"Good girl. Waiting for me."

"Yes, Sir."

And then he drove up into her with such force that her eyes rolled back in her head and she almost came on the spot. He held her down on his cock for a second, making her feel everything inside her. His hardness, the cool intrusive plug and it was all so so so much.

He grabbed her hair and pulled her down to kiss her hard. "I love you."

"I love you too, Sir."

Only then did he let her move upwards, pushing her up until she came off his cock with a very loud, very long release of air.

Silence.

And then he gave a roar of laughter and pulled her straight back down onto his cock. "Oh Buttercup, you sweet sweet thing."

She buried her head in his shoulder, "It's not funny!"

"It's kinda of funny."

"Well maybe, Sir." She paused, and then found herself giggling. "It was pretty loud."

"Pretty loud?!"

"Fine, yes. The loudest pussy fart that there's ever been." But she was smiling through her blushes.

"A queenly queef."

She went to hit him but he moved against her and she gasped instead.

"Don't be embarrassed, it's my fault for going in too hard." She muttered something under her breath at his words, and he chucked under her chin, "What was that?"

"It wasn't too hard, Sir."

"Oh no?" His eyes glinted and he moved up against her. "Sit up then, Buttercup; let's see how this feels." And then he started thrusting upwards.

Hard.

Before it had been full on; now, with her arse clenching around the butt plug, and her pussy clenching around his cock, it was her whole world. Nothing existed outside this.

His cock, hitting her g-spot in just the right position, over and over again, her body arching up and she had to brace herself with her hands against his legs behind her.

"Touch yourself."

"Pardon, Sir?"

"Touch. Yourself."

And so she did.

She leaned forward so that she could rest her forehead against his as he pounded into to her over and over, and reached down with one hand to play with her clit again.

If she had been close when he'd been fucking her doggy style, now she could feel the waves of her encroaching orgasm crashing against her. And she kept herself there, riding the edge, for as long as she could, playing with her clit and then backing off before she tipped over, again and again. In a continuous loop of lust until she was so slick with desire that she wasn't sure where she ended and he began.

He nudged her head up and kissed her, biting her lip sharply. "You still with me, Buttercup?"

"Yes, Sir." The words were automatic, automated.

"Buttercup?"

"Please, Sir, I…please can I?"

"Of course, sweetness. Come apart for me."

She wasn't sure whether it was the final flick against her clit, or the extra thrust of his cock, but she found herself spiralling into a waterfall; desire hammering through her body, making her spasm in pleasure, every part of her tight and loose simultaneously. It sounded as if the world was shattering and she felt completely spent.

And she was suddenly empty, vaguely aware of him gently laying her down, and checking her over.

She was very sleepy. "Did you come, Sir?"

He chuckled and lay down behind her, pulling her close, "I'm more concerned about you, love. Does your arse feel okay?"

"My arse?" She was confused and then, when she realised that her arse was empty, even more confused. "What? Did you take it out? I…?" He shook so hard, that she turned to look at him and was surprised to see him laughing. "What's so funny?"

He pointed across the room to where a picture frame on the dresser was shattered, and her glass butt plug – miraculously intact – lay next to it. "You came a little…enthusiastically."

She was no longer sleepy. "Wait, what? Are you saying that I-"

"Came so hard that your butt plug shot out of your arse and smashed a picture frame? Yes, yes I am."

She blinked. "Wow. My arse is powerful."

"I'd actually argue that it was the orgasm that was powerful, and I think I had a little something to do with that."

She rolled her eyes, and snuggled up back against him. "I mean, I feel fine, so you know, just another disaster in a night of disasters."

Leaning on his elbow, he sat up, tugging her round to look at him. "Near disasters. None of those were disasters."

"No? I fell over during my striptease. You got a cramp in the middle of sex. I did the loudest pussy fart known to man, and then my butt plug went rogue."

He leaned in and kissed her. It wasn't the hard passionate kiss of frenzied fucking; this was sweet and gentle and kind. "Yes, but none of those were actual disasters, sweetness. We laughed; they were funny, if a little embarrassing. But I want to always shatter picture frames with butt plugs with you. I always want this with you. I always want us."

"I want that too." She kissed him this time, and put all of her heart and soul and Buttercup-ness into it.

When he pulled back, she was a little confused, but he kissed her forehead, and then reached down to grab something from one of the drawers beside the bed. "Sweetness, I love you. Will you, please, be mine?"

Looking down, she saw a jewellery box open, and inside the most delicate silver choker that she'd ever seen. A single band with a tiny lock at the back. A collar. In that moment she felt everything that she felt for him come flooding over her: their easy love; their trust in each other; their laughter over awkward moments; and the fact that, no matter what, they always carried on. Together.

She turned around and lifted her hair up so he could fix it about her neck and do it up. The metal was cool against her skin and felt like a kiss.

"I was already yours. And I always will be."

TURNING ON

$\mathcal{T}$he beach was surprisingly quiet for a Sunday evening.

The weekend warriors had left for home, and all that was left were a few locals, sitting, relaxing, having a few beers. And seagulls. There were always seagulls on the beach.

But it was still quiet in the only way that really mattered, that echo deep down in her soul that meant that the sounds of the sea brought stillness.

She'd had to put in some extra hours that Saturday, to keep on top of an ever-expanding workload, and when it was done her girlfriend had practically pushed her out the door.

She wasn't annoyed about that; if anything, she was kind of grateful for the fact that her girlfriend knew her well enough to know when she needed fresh air, and also when she needed to be on her own.

Not permanently, of course.

Just for a short while.

A short moment, on her own, with no voices breaking her calm.

She tripped her way down the shingled beach, wobbling

over pebbles and tiny, crushed up, bits of shell beneath her flipflops. Trip trip, all the way down to where the waves met the shore with that swishing noise of stones being pushed forwards and dragged backwards over each other.

Closing her eyes, she stood there, face turned towards the sea. Listening.

There was something about the sea, that much she knew. It caught her unawares sometimes, the impact of that vastness, stretching out as far as the eye could see. It wasn't that it made her feel insignificant exactly, but rather that she felt connected to something bigger. The breadth and depth and moreness that made her feel comfortable with who she was.

Opening her eyes, she moved to sit down, squirming her arse until she found a comfortable spot amongst the pebbles.

Ah.

She'd needed this. Needed to physically get up and walk away from all of *that*. She lay back, lacing her fingers together behind her head, and took a deep breath. The tang of salt filled her senses, the sounds of the sea washing over her. Soothing her. Excellent. An evening like this was perfect. Half an hour on the beach, cuddles on the sofa at home, and then bed. Sleep.

Maybe.

She hadn't been sleeping. Tossing and turning all night, incapable of settling into some kind of space, and it was starting to have an effect. Making her short-tempered at work and cross with herself, which in itself was exhausting. And so the cycle begun again.

By the time she made her way back home, it was dinnertime, and the front door opened on a picturesque scene, her girlfriend framed in the entrance to the kitchen as she twirled around, singing along to some song on the radio.

It made her laugh to see her love there, the folds of her skirt drifted like petals dancing on a breeze. So much joy in those flowing movements, head rocked back as she sung out, then back forwards to check on the steaks in the pan.

"Dinner's up in just a moment!"

"I'm sorry I-"

"No." Her girlfriend cut her off. "You've been working so damn hard; you needed the break. And the sea always makes you feel better."

That was true, but it didn't make her feel any less guilty for leaving her other half with the cooking. "I'll cook tomorrow night."

The smile that answered her suggestion warmed her. "That would be lovely."

Time to clean up, wash away the salt that had transferred from pebbles to her hands, and lay the table.

She put out a candle, patchouli and sandalwood, soft scents to accompany dinner and even grabbed the fancy napkins, before pouring a glass of water and settling in her seat.

Her girlfriend practically danced into the room, balancing plates and then placing them carefully on the placemats. "Eat up!"

She eyed her cautiously. "What's up with you?"

"Nothing!"

That was too quick and easy a response. Her girlfriend never answered a question with one word. "Hmmmmm..." She cut into her steak, and snuck a look at the woman sat across the table from her. She was sat there, fiddling with the scarf around her neck, and almost vibrating with energy. "Okay, come on, what's the matter?"

"Nothing's the matter as such..." Her girlfriend took a gulp from her glass and almost spluttered it everywhere. "Okay, well, how would you like to play tonight?"

"Play?"

"We haven't in a while, and it might help you sleep better."

Playing was fun, that much was certainly true. She'd been too tired the last few weeks to do anything other than pass out in bed at the end of the day, too drained of energy, of life. And it was hard when she felt like that.

Frankly, she hated it.

The playfulness that they engaged in brought her respite, and she suddenly realised that she needed it. Wanted it.

"Okay, it sounds like a plan."

Her mind began racing; what to do, how to play... So many choices from which to choose. And all of them at their fingertips. It was almost overwhelming; too many options. And she wanted it. But she wanted to be good. Needed to be good.

After dinner, she did the washing up; the routine soothing her, settling her mindset before she could follow her girlfriend up the stairs into an evening of fun. Wash up, put away, tidy up. And she found her mind wandering, away from her waiting girlfriend upstairs, and more towards the door of her office, and the work she'd been so determined to put aside for one evening.

But everything seemed slower. More drawn out. Not a bad thing, just-

Different.

Drying her hands slowly on the tea towel, she walked to the bottom of the stairs, and stood there, momentarily frozen.

Detachment wasn't her thing. She was all about enthusiastic consent on both sides and right now she felt disparate. Not fully present.

Steeling herself, she strode up the staircase, taking the steps two at a time in her confusion. She'd explain. It would be fine. Her girlfriend would understand and-

oh.

Oh.

As she walked into their room, her girlfriend was standing with her back to the door, that skirt fluttering lightly around her kissable thighs and in her hands was rope.

Rope.

"You've been so stressed, my love." Her girlfriend didn't turn to look at her as she entered, just continued to unravel and disentangle the knots in the purple cotton. "So, I thought perhaps we could switch it up tonight. What do you think?"

The sigh of relief she let out was louder than she'd expected and she sagged against the wall. "Oh. Yes please Miss." For a moment, she thought she would cry.

Her girlfriend usually lent towards submission, and her domination, but both of them enjoyed swapping roles on occasion. And right now, submitting, emptying her head and just following sounded ideal.

The sunshiney smile that her girlfriend sent her made her glow. "Good girl. Now, why don't you get undressed for me and go stand by the wardrobe."

"Yes, Miss." Slowly, she made her way to the side of the bed, taking off one item of clothing, and then another, folding them and putting them neatly on her chair. She kind of liked slow when she was subbing, taking her time, letting her body relax into this state of not quite being in control.

Not quite, because everything was suggestions when her girlfriend was in charge. No 'you must do this' or 'follow my orders', just gentle suggestions that would be rewarded with a soft word of praise that made her feel like she'd a climb a mountain if her girlfriend asked. And she was not a climbing mountains kind of woman.

She liked that.

She liked the fact that she wasn't going to be barked at, and that accidentally doing something wrong and getting told off was off the table. This was low stress kink, and it was perfect for her.

Walking over to the wardrobe, she snuck a peek at her girlfriend.

Miss hadn't changed, as she often didn't when she was Domming. There was something exhilarating about the fact that her girlfriend could flit around in her pretty summer dress, all sweet and adorable and unassuming, when all she wanted to do was fall to her knees in worship.

"I'd rather you looked towards the wall please."

See? Suggestions.

She heard the swish of a skirt as Miss walked up behind her, and then went on tiptoes to whisper in her ear, the words a caress of their own. "Safe word?"

"Rapunzel. Yours, Miss?"

"Adventure."

It wasn't as if they didn't already know each other's safe words, but that was part of the routine. Part of slipping into whichever role they were taking on. The Domme asked first, the sub asked second, and it let them know where they stood.

Miss dropped a kiss onto her bare shoulder before walking away.

Her absence left a draught, the cool air against her skin making her shiver.

The lights turned off, and then a warm glow just within her peripheral vision, came from where their lamp sat.

And then Miss was back, and she had the rope with her.

Rope had a very distinctive sound. People didn't always understand that. The slide of flaxen cotton over skin, over the palms of her girlfriend's hands, couldn't be mistaken. And it sent her hurtling into subspace.

This time, when she closed her eyes, it wasn't to wonder at the sound of the sea, or to listen to the pebbles shucked along the beach; it was to hear the promise in the rope.

You will be still.

She longed to be still, and the rope would get her there. Miss would get her there.

The first loop slipped over her head, and she felt Miss make a knot in the hollow below her neck. Solid. This was solid. Another knot, and then around her back and that was the moment when she kind of stopped focusing on anything other than the feel of the flax, soft against her skin. And those brief, teasing touches, each time Miss brushed against her, intent on nothing but the ropework.

She liked this.

Liked the fact that at that moment *she*, with all her crowded thoughts and fears and stresses, didn't really matter. Not really. What mattered was that she was solid. That she was still. That she was the perfect canvas for Miss to tie up in any which way She wanted.

A tap on her thigh and she spread her legs, waiting for the inevitable kiss of knot to her clit.

There.

And then the rope was under and up, tracing her spine until it ducked beneath the loop around her neck.

Her arms would be next.

And then her wrists.

Cotton on her wrists sent her deeper, the sound of her breathing evening out until she felt so still, arms pulled back, the heel of her palms kissing above the restraints.

She never wanted to be fully immobile because there was something quite delicious in choosing this for herself. In the same way that she loved that Miss always made suggestions, as opposed to giving orders.

It was something that Miss loved about her submission; that she wanted to submit. That she wanted to please.

For she really did. She wanted that pleasure of knowing that, even if only for a few moments, her submission empowered her partner. It was her gift to Miss.

"Well don't you look pretty?"

A finger beneath her chin made her open her eyes and blink rapidly. Those smiling lips were close to hers, and Miss leaned in to snatch a kiss before stepping back to admire Her handiwork.

"So very very pretty. Would you like to see?"

There was a pause there; this was an actual question, not rhetorical. It needed answering.

"It's okay if you don't want to see right now." Miss came close, and then it was her girlfriend's cheek against hers, warm, comforting. Partner as well as Domme. "I promise."

"I-I would like to see. Please. Miss."

A hand slipped in the small gap between her arm and side, and manoeuvred her round so that she could see herself in the mirror, her diminutive Miss standing behind her.

She didn't study herself in the mirror very often. A glance to check her hair, or to apply some makeup, but standing and looking? Really looking? No. Not something she did.

But she did now.

The woman standing opposite her, mirroring her, was flushed. That was the first thing she noticed, that her flushed skin looked pretty bound up against the soft violet of the rope. And then the rope itself, lines intersecting, criss-crossing across her body. Plump curves spilled around those lines, and as she moved, turning this way and that, the rope tightened and loosened. Indenting her body with firm, unrelenting pressure.

She loved it.

Her eyes caught on the purple diamond over her breastbone. It sat there, framed by her heavy breasts, shoulders back, hands hidden behind her, and she'd never felt prettier.

"I look like art, Miss."

The sudden sparkle in Miss' eyes made her feel like she'd said the right thing. "Art?"

She blushed, and watched in the mirror, fascinated, as the pink painted her skin. "I mean-"

"No no." Miss interrupted her and leaned in with a wicked grin that made her immediately wonder whether she'd made the right decision. "I agree. You do look like art."

"Thank you, Miss."

"You're very welcome, but I don't think that statues talk."

She shot Her a wide-eyed look, but Miss took her chin in hand and firmly turned her head back to look in the mirror.

"Yes, statues definitely don't usually speak. Unless they need to safe out?"

Their eyes met in the mirror, and she gave a small shake of the head. No. She didn't need to safe out.

"And statues also don't move. A freeze frame."

Gazes met in the mirror once more, and she blinked once. Twice.

A warmth touched her cheek in a kiss and she had to stop herself from melting into it.

"I've never had such a wonderful piece of art." Miss began to circle her slowly. Talking all the while. "I watch you sometimes, darting from task to task, rarely pausing, rarely stopping. And I think you rather like being still, don't you?" There was a gurgle of laughter as silence met Her question. "Oh you *are* good at this. How wonderful!"

She didn't move her gaze from the mirror, eyes focused just over Miss' shoulder as she felt a single finger run along her collarbone, tugging gently at the knot as it passed over it. Her nipples tightened and she felt her clit twitch.

"I wonder what I should do with you. Perhaps I should place you where I can see you. Lean back and appreciate each curve as I stroke myself."

Her cunt tightened at the thought of Miss masturbating whilst *she* remained unable to do anything other than stand

and look across the room, praying for a glimpse of that perfection out the corner of her eye.

"That would be entertaining, and art is meant to entertain, for sure."

The finger moved down to her nipple and caught it in a tight pinch.

She fought not to gasp.

"Or maybe I should study this statue up close. Evaluate each and every minute detail."

Miss traced the rope up and round each breast and then followed it down til She paused, just hovering over the knot on her clit. "What happens if I tug this, I wonder?" Miss' face moved close, as if determined to catalogue every tiny movement, and she felt complete stillness wash over her.

She was no longer *her*.

Was she a statue, a sculpture?

She didn't know.

All she knew was that she just *was*.

It was as if she'd floated up, out of her body, until she could look down at this perfect sculpture, moulded by and for Miss. There for Her pleasure, and no one else's.

Fuck. She was free.

She felt Miss tug at the rope, felt the knot pull against her clit, knew how wet she was, but still she didn't move.

Miss' delight was clear, and it meant something to her, in the space where she floated.

"Do you think that statues can come?" Then words whispered more intensely. "I'm not sure that they can."

And then Her fingers were slipping beneath the rope to tease at her slick entrance, and flickering against the nub of her clit.

All she could think was 'statues don't come, statues don't come', over and over, a desperate pleading to herself to stay here, in this stillness. A sharp tug against the rope and she felt the flax against the cleft of her arse, another knot she hadn't yet noticed, suddenly rubbing up against her rosebud, and then Miss' fingers were inside her, filling her over and over. In and out, the tips of Her fingers grazing against her g-spot and she felt her body flush.

Her desire was apparent now in the wet sounds that came with the finger fucking, and when Miss pulled her fingers out to look, wetness followed. That delighted laugh again, and then silence as She tasted her. Licked Her fingers clean, and then thrust them straight back in, and she thought that that might be the thing that pushed her over the edge.

It didn't though, because this time the thrust was accompanied by a sharp slap to her left breast.

Her breast jiggled.

She did not move.

And she definitely didn't come.

"What a good statue you are."

Miss moved around her and then pulled until she stumbled backwards, until her calves touched the bed. She felt the mattress move and then Miss move her bound hands, her fingers pointing horizontally out behind her.

More movement behind her, more of the mattress moving and she wanted to look, wanted to see, but statues don't move. Statues don't move.

Something at the tip of her fingertips. Wet. Slick.

Oh. My.

That was Miss' pussy.

She kept herself entirely still, determined not to move a muscle, as Miss moved against her, fucking Herself on her fingers. Each movement threatened to shatter the stone stillness she'd built up inside, but she needed this. Needed to be solid. Needed to be exactly what *Miss* needed. And that meant staying exactly as she was.

Her fingers slid in and out of that warm tightness and she

knew that her own pussy was just as wet, just as slick, but still her fingers remained motionless, allowing Miss to take what she needed. Take her pleasure from her perfect statue.

Never had being art felt more glorious.

And she'd never been art like this before.

She could tell when Miss was going to come. It was in the hitch of Her breathing, the tightening of Her pussy, and in the words that danced from Her tongue. "I love you. My perfect statue. Still for no one but me. No one but me. My statue. Mine. Oh-" and then words stopped altogether as She spasmed around her fingers.

If she was the perfect statue, then She was life itself. Effervescent. A fountain bubbling over.

When Miss had come down from the dizzying heights that she'd clearly been residing in, she stumbled round to stand between her and the mirror again.

Her dress was askew, one strap fallen down past one shoulder, and Her skin was damp with a sheen of sweat.

She longed to lick Miss' skin.

But still she remained statue.

"So, do statues come?"

Silence.

Miss popped up onto Her tiptoes and kissed her cheek. "Permission to speak granted, statue. Consider it a boon after pleasing me so."

She swallowed, wetting her lips. "Statues don't come, Miss."

Miss blinked and then it was her girlfriend who smiled softly at her. "They don't?"

"No, Miss. They don't. And I want to be a good statue." She liked the stillness, the way that this longing painted her desire in broad brushstrokes, how it kept her mind quiet. And she wasn't ready to let go of that just yet. "I want to be a good statue for you."

A glass of water was lifted to her lips, and she drank gratefully.

"You *are* a good statue for me." There was a pause and then her girlfriend asked, "Do you want to come?"

She cast her eyes downwards, the only movement in her otherwise unmoving body.

"Ah." And the as swiftly as she disappeared, Miss was back. "It's Sunday tomorrow love, and I don't think I'm done playing with my art. How about we see if paintings can come tomorrow?"

She breathed her acquiescence out. "Yes. *Please.*" And then "Thank you, Miss." She loved her girlfriend.

HITTING ON

She was back again.

It had to be her.

No one else's shoes made quite such a distinctive clip clip clip sound. In fact, the sound of most people's footfall was deadened by the terrible acoustics in the library, but *somehow* hers managed to remain distinct. The only sharp sound in a chorus of hushed muttering.

He pressed pause on reshelving some science fiction to sneak a look around the corner of the bookshelves. Yup. That was her. Sat at the same table as ever, high ponytail swaying from side to side as she leant down to her bag to take out her notebook.

The first time she'd come in, it had been a Tuesday. He remembered that because it had also been 'Books with Tots' which he usually avoided like the plague, but on that Tuesday he'd been roped into covering for the resident children's librarian.

'Books with Tots' meant nursery rhymes and that adorable *Julián is a Mermaid* book, but also sticky fingers and lots of crying, and children clambering all over the place and wanting hugs and though – *ugh*, sticky fingers – he wasn't *heartless*. He wasn't going to turn them away. So there he was, trying his utmost to turn chaos into a nice serene reading group, and when he looked up, there she was.

Long blonde hair swooped up high in a ponytail, plaid shirt paired with blue jeans, and this look on her face as if she couldn't quite work out what to make of him.

He'd been about to roll his eyes at the chaos surrounding him, when some rapscallion of a toddler rugby tackled him around the neck and he faceplanted onto the beanbag especially selected for this session.

There was a short, throaty chuckle, but when he finally managed to disentangle himself from the would be rugby player she was gone, and he found himself feeling vaguely disappointed.

The next time she'd visited, he hadn't even realised that she was there until she dumped a towering pile of books on the checkout desk with a thump.

They'd been trying out a few new displays – 'BookTok' in the YA section, and 'SpicyTok' at the very back of the adult section – and he recognised some, if not most of these from the latter as he scanned them.

"Oh," he'd said when he scanned one with a bondage-lite cover.

"Oh?"

He'd stumbled over his words then. "I mean, interesting… no, I…that looks, I-" He gave up, ducking his head and abandoning any attempt at conversation.

"Oh wow, you really are just too precious, aren't you?"

Her head was slightly on one side and she looked as if there was a smile lurking just behind her eyes.

"I, er…" Then he realised in a panic that she might have taken his words as a come on. "I'm so sorry, whatever you want to read is-"

"It's okay," she started placing her books in a tote bag, before slinging it over her shoulder, "I know what you meant. You weren't being inappropriate."

His sigh of relief brought a glint of amusement back to her eyes.

"Okay Mr Appropriate, I'll see you next time."

And after that she'd become a regular. The same table, tucked away behind the reference section, every Tuesday at the same time for three hours. She'd grab her notebook, pull out whichever book she was reading, and intensely take notes for the entire duration. She barely ever looked up, unless it was to head towards the romance section to grab another book.

But at the end of her session, every week, he made sure he was standing at the checkout desk.

Most people used the newer checkout machines, but she never did. She always walked straight towards him, never deviating from her path, her gaze never moving from his face.

At first it was almost a dare, but she soon seemed to realise that it didn't matter what she did, she was always going to win. He couldn't help it, being the first one to break eye contact, that inevitable flush staining his cheeks as he looked down, and then there'd be that huff of a chuckle that he felt all the way down in his-

Well. Yes.

She couldn't be oblivious to the effect she was having on him. In fact, he was fairly certain that she was hitting on him, but he didn't quite know what to do with that piece of information, and so instead each week he checked out her books for her, and allowed himself stolen glances at her face as she studied him, that almost smile curving her lips.

Once he'd asked her if she would like to order any books in, almost defiantly meeting her eyes, and she'd risen to the challenge, giving him such a list that his face heated almost immediately and he'd bitten his lip to stop himself from making any kind of sound. To admitting that her teasing was having an indelible effect on him.

She'd leaned on the desk that time, one hand casually tapping the top and each tap felt like each clip of her heels every time she entered the library. Like she was knocking on *his* door, demanding *his* attention, even though she wasn't doing anything of the sort.

But when he read back to her the name of the titles she was ordering in, he made himself meet her eyes and give a half smile back of his own.

It had been worth it, because she'd softened then, the cocky almost smile melting into a real one and she'd opened her mouth to say something before she stopped herself. "I do actually need to order these books, you know? It's not just-"

"An attempt to make me blush?" His words sounded more confident than he felt, but she smiled and nodded.

"Exactly, my research is based around..." she waved her hand in the general direction of his computer, where a variety of BDSM and kink-related titles were typed out. "Well, you can see for yourself."

"I can indeed."

The half-smile she offered him was practically shy, and he smiled back, a grin throwing itself across his face. "Well, until next week then?"

"Until next week."

And the week after, and the week after.

On Tuesday mornings he became almost unbearably chirpy, bouncing around until she arrived, when he simmered down and just waited until their checkout conversation. And last week? Last week they'd ended up talking for almost fifteen minutes about a graphic novel that she'd picked up, and she'd said nonchalantly – so damn nonchalant that it had clearly been planned – "It would be cool to chat to someone about this kind of stuff regularly. None of my friends are really into comics," and then she'd picked up her books and left without even looking at him. And perhaps, just perhaps, there might have been a blush staining *her* cheeks this time.

He realised that he was going to have to make the first official move. She might have posited a scenario, but it was fairly certain that her walking out immediately afterwards was her way of not pressuring him, of letting him know that if he wanted to, that would be cool, but that she didn't want to make him feel uncomfortable.

So, this week he was going to see if she'd be interested in going for coffee. No pressure or strings, just coffee.

And so he stood there, *Kindred* in hand, working up the courage to go and speak to her. He could do this. He could. He should because he liked her and she clearly liked him and damn it why wouldn't his legs just *move*?!

One small step. Another small step. And then a couple of them in a row until he rounded her table and cleared his throat quietly.

"Hmmm?" She looked up, her eyes briefly, adorably, cross-eyed until she blinked, refocusing on him. "Oh, hey."

"Hey."

There was a pause in which she raised her eyebrows in question.

"Coffee." Sentences were apparently out of the question.

"Coffee?"

"Coffee."

"Dark brown bitter drink, usually drunk hot?"

"Shit, I mean, would you like to have coffee? With me. Sometime."

And there was that bemused almost smile and then the

half-smile and then this dazzling full-on actual smile. "Coffee sounds lovely. Do you get a lunch break?"

"Yes."

"Tomorrow? Around noon?"

He nodded, relieved that his part was now done.

"Cool, I'll meet you out front then."

Another nod and he hovered there, feeling awkward before she shooed him away. "Go back to work, I've got studying to do."

"Oh, of course!" and then he was back shelving science fiction novels, grinning happily to himself.

The following day was bracing. A brisk wind only kept at bay by a warm coat and the hat, scarf and gloves his Nana had knitted for him. He pulled the hat down over his ears, buried his chin in the scarf, and shoved his hands in his pockets whilst he waited. He'd taken an extra-long lunch – he was owed some extra time as he often forgot and found himself working through – and besides, it meant he'd have more time with her.

That frisson of excitement fizzed and he hopped from foot to foot, keeping an eye out for her.

Soon enough, she rounded the corner of the street, and he had to take a deep breath because she looked so damn *her*. Ear muffs covered her ears, allowing her ponytail to hang free, cheeks and nose rosy from the cold, and her jacket was leather, oversized on her frame, but it was her confident stride towards him that made him catch his breath.

He didn't know how she could walk like that whilst wearing heeled boots – he was sure that he'd have tripped and fallen – but she just strode on over, each step bringing her closer until she was smiling at him, amusement in her eyes.

"Cold?"

He humphed and his breath huffed out in a cloud, "A little."

"Well let's head across to that café over there then, and get out of the cold." She pointed across the road, and he found himself following her obediently.

He insisted on opening the door for her though, a gesture that was somewhat spoiled by the fact that his scarf got caught in it when he let it close behind him, and he got yanked backwards with an "Oof."

It wasn't too dignified, sitting on his arse on the floor, but she'd offered him a hand with a smile, and checked that he was okay, before picking out a table for them to sit at.

"Shall we get a panini or sumat too?" she asked. "If you've time, of course."

"I've two hours, so I've plenty of time."

She furrowed her brow, "Wow, I should be a librarian! I want two hour lunch breaks!"

"Oh no," he hurried to reassure her, "That's just cos I always forget to take lunch; I've got plenty of overtime."

And then there was that look again, the one as if she wanted to say something, but didn't quite know how it'd be received.

"What is it? Is everything okay?"

He watched, concerned as she blinked once, twice, and then nodded firmly, as if she'd decided something. "Be honest with me?"

"Always."

"Why did you ask me out for coffee?"

It was at that moment that the waitress came to take their order, and he couldn't have been more grateful for the brief respite because there were a million ways in which he could answer that. And a million ways in which he wouldn't.

"Well?"

He looked up when the waitress left and went for the

most acceptable explanation. "You said that you wanted to talk about comic books with someone..." His voice trailed off as she lifted an eyebrow.

"Okay," she said slowly. "Let's try that again; and this time I'd like the real reason please."

Her voice, that voice, hit him deep in his solar plexus and the words were dragged out from him before he even realised that he was speaking. "You seem to know. What I'm thinking, that is. And you're smart and hot and you like books. I think we'd have things to talk about." His sentences stuttered, disjointed and short, and he was grateful for the steamy mug of hot chocolate that landed in front of him. Perfect. That way he didn't have to look at her. Didn't have to meet her eyes and see her response.

There was a chuckle from across the table, and then silence as she took a sip from her own coffee.

More silence.

Ack. Well, he'd somehow managed to make it fucking awkward and now all he wanted to do was gather up his coat, scarf and all other extraneous knitted items and throw himself back out onto the mercy of the biting cold outside.

"Hey," the voice that interrupted his musings was quiet. Gentle.

A hand crept across the table and nudged his once, and then again, a little more urgently when he didn't look up.

"Hmmmm?" He finally raised his head, but still looked anywhere but at her.

"Okay," she said. Her voice firm this time, and his eyes snapped to her without him meaning to. "If we're going to...hang out, then you need to communicate a little better with me. It's okay to be nervous and unsure, but it's not okay not to explain what the matter is. That's important."

"Yes Mi-" He froze, panic clawing the word back as fast as it could. "Ah, I mean-"

"It's okay, just maybe not yet? Not til we've talked some more?" There was that gentleness again, as if she knew that he needed to be reassured and petted and handled with the softest of kid gloves. "Not that hearing that title would be anything but delightful, coming from your lips, but I kind of need to earn it first. For now, why don't we eat and talk and see if we like each other as much as our brief interactions at the library have indicated."

He nodded, relieved that she hadn't freaked out, that he hadn't completely misread the situation, and kind of grateful for the reprieve. He wanted this, *her* – that had been clear from the first time she'd laughed at him – but he'd been burnt before, fallen too quickly into a dynamic that had left him scalded and shy. Getting to know each other made sense.

And so they did. They sat and ate and talked about books and life and the more they spoke, the more comfortable he felt. She felt it too; he could tell. Burst of sunshine every time a true smile broke through that bemused mask that sat on her face, and then glimpses of that other her, the one who he longed to obey, just behind the curtain.

When they'd finished and paid, she'd stood up first, offering her hand casually to him, and when he slipped his hand into hers, it felt like the most natural thing ever.

Outside the cafe, across the road from the library, they'd stood together, hands intertwined and he couldn't stop grinning, couldn't stop from peeking at her. Her huff of laughter let him know that she'd noticed.

"I like you," he blurted out. "And I'd like to see you again. Romantically. Not just for coffee."

She reached out and took his other hand, and they faced each other, the wind whistling past their faces, painting them red. "I'd like that very much. But-" There was another of those pregnant pauses, ones with so much at stake, only this time the pause didn't linger. "Look, I'm pretty kinky, and that's an important dynamic in a relationship for me. Now, from what you said earlier," she smiled at his sudden shyness, "you might be kinky too. But it's important to get that stuff sorted, discussed."

"A negotiation?"

Her relief at his words was apparent. "Exactly. I'd like to keep seeing you, but a negotiation and setting of expectations seems sensible before I-" and here she stumbled over her words a bit, "before we get entangled further. I like you, but I've been hurt before and-"

He squeezed her hands and stepped forward, scanning her face to make sure that it was okay. "I think that sounds like a very good idea. Thank you for being so forthright. And responsible."

Her satisfied sigh filled him with pleasure. He'd made her feel like that, comfortable and happy. He wanted to do it again.

"When are you free? For the negotiation?"

"You are eager, aren't you?" She looked as if she wanted to say something more, but she stopped and took a breath. "Maybe one evening after work this week?"

"Yes please."

"And where would you like to meet?"

Location was important, he knew that. Public, so that if they decided not to move forward, there was no awkwardness, but also relatively quiet. Plus there was the safety aspect; he wanted her to feel comfortable. "There's a pub near here that has lots of tucked away corners, the King Alfred. I could book a booth?"

"That would work perfectly. Though no drinking during negotiations."

"Of course not, though," he added, "I might be a little shy."

She beamed up at him then. "That's okay, I like shy." Then, "Do you want to kiss me?"

"Oh, yes please." He could honestly say that there was nothing he wanted more in that moment. His gaze dropped to where her lips curved invitingly, but he stayed there, waiting.

"Oh aren't you good, waiting for me!" she said impulsively and he flushed as she beckoned him closer with a crook of her finger. "You may indeed kiss me."

She'd barely finished what she'd said before he leaned down to meet those lips with his. They were soft, pliable, and he moaned instinctively before delving deeper, his hands moving to cup her face as he showed her everything of himself. She nipped at his lip and he felt his cock twitch before she moved back, looking as flushed as he felt.

"Well, well, Mr Appropriate can certainly kiss."

His laugh was loud in the relative quiet of the road, only lone cars passing them by, and he scrunched up his face a little. "So can you."

"Oh, I know. So, when would you-"

"Tomorrow? If you're free?"

Her hand reached up to caress his cheek briefly, and she nodded. "Tomorrow. You'll book the pub? It's close?"

"On this road. And they do food too, if you'd like to eat together again."

"It's always a good idea to keep your strength up during negotiations." This time, her smile was a wicked promise and he blinked rapidly, trying to compose himself. "Go on, go back to work. I'll pick you up after your shift tomorrow. Six o'clock?"

"Half past; got to do the clean up once the library closes."

"Sure. Tomorrow then," and without another look behind her, she walked off. He stood there, watching her leave, completely entranced by the swing of her hips and that confident stride that so encapsulated her, before turning back to work.

And the following day he was all over the place.

He was louder than usual, his voice rebounding around the library, to his colleagues' amusement, and instead of reshelving sensibly, one genre at a time, he bounced all over the place with his cart – flitting from section to section, almost staggering to a stop each time he thought of her.

When the last patrons of the library had left, he zoomed around, finishing up everything so early that he had nothing to do for the last twenty minutes before she arrived but wait. He wished he'd had thought to ask for her number, to let her know that he was done early, but instead he found himself walking over to her chair, and sitting on the floor beside it, leaning back against reference shelves that surely could have found a definition for how he was feeling. Because he wasn't sure. It wasn't quite excitement and it wasn't quite nervousness; something in between.

Closing his eyes, he imagined her voice, the scritch of her pencil on paper, and he thought about what it would feel like to sit at her feet. His breathing slowed and he allowed his heart rate, that had been racing all day, to settle into the idea of it.

It was very nice.

So he sat there, allowing himself to drift in and out of daydreams, until his alarm went off, startling him up onto his feet.

One last glance, one last check that the computers were off and there wasn't anything lying around that could send the library and all its books up in flames, and then he was out the front door, locking it behind him.

"Perfectly on time." Her voice was warm and he had to fight not to melt then and there, by the side of the road. She turned her head to the side, offering him her cheek. "If you'd like to kiss me?"

"Yes." One word and then his lips were brushing the softness of her skin, once, twice before he pulled himself up, blushing all the while.

She grinned at him. "I love the feel of stubble."

His eyes darted left and right and she gurgled with laughter, "Oh sweetheart, come on, let's go to the pub. We can talk more there."

The King Alfred pub had been around for as long as he could remember, way back into his childhood, and had been a haunt of his in his early twenties. But it still appealed now, the wood panelling adding a cosy intimacy to the ambience; exactly what was needed for two kinky thirty-somethings looking for a little privacy.

They'd stopped at the bar in the centre of the room, to grab menus that they'd come back to order from, and a soft drink each – lemonade for him and mango juice for her – before making their way to the booth in the back that seemed tucked away from prying eyes.

He stopped to let her slide in first and then sat opposite her.

She took out a notebook and he snorted lemonade out of his nose.

"You're going to take notes?"

"If that's okay?"

He paused for a moment, "Can I ask why?"

"Of course!" she smiled at him reassuringly. "I've ADHD so we could talk forever, but that doesn't mean that I'd take any of it in. I probably won't just by making notes, but having them means that if we decide to move forward, then I can sit and reread them before we meet up, to make sure that I don't forget anything important." She stopped and thought for a moment. "If we ever decide to stop or not to move forward, I'll give them back to you. If that works?"

He nodded his acquiescence and she smiled and nodded back, taking a long sip of her drink before flipping open the pad and retrieving a mechanical pencil from somewhere in her bag.

"Okay, how would you like to start?"

He blinked rapidly. He'd done negotiations before, but it had usually been led by the Domme. "Me?"

"Yup, this is sumat we're doing together hun, and I want us to be comfortable together, so you lead."

"Oh, okay. Hard limits?"

"Always a good start."

He stalled by taking another sip of his lemonade, thinking hard. He was pretty chilled most of the time; usually happy to try most things but... "I suppose no scat, watersports, knives or CBT."

She nodded vigorously. "Yeah, none of those are for me either, so that's a good start. What else?" She met his eyes across the table and frowned. "You know you have to be upfront with me, right? No holding back, at least, not when it comes to limits. If there are kinks you don't want to talk about now, that's fine, that can come with time, but being honest about limits? That's non-negotiable; for my wellbeing as much as your own."

Swallowing, he nodded and then muttered hoarsely, "I don't like being humiliated. Teased? Sure. But humiliated and insulted and told that I'm worthless-" His throat closed up and he tapped three times on the table sharply.

She immediately put her pen down and jumped. "I'll grab some water. Bubbles might not help right now lovely."

He was vaguely aware of her walking away but focused in on his breathing. In. Out. In. Out. In for four. Out for four. In for four. Out for four.

By the time she returned, his breathing had evened out and he was able to nod his thanks.

"Would you like to stop?" Her words were calm, and

completely free of the accusatory tone he'd feared hearing. "It's okay if you-"

"No. Please. I just-it's a hard limit for a reason."

She nodded slowly and mumbled something under her breath.

"What?"

A huff and then she said slowly and firmly, "I hope I never meet the person who put that look in your eyes."

Her words felt like armour, and they slotted into place around him, drawing him closer to her. "You won't. They're not in my life anymore."

"That sounds like it was a good decision to make." Her words were tight. "Shitty exes fuck us up so much; so bound-arying is important. Well done. My hard limits include what you mentioned earlier, crops – I can't bear the sound they make – and being expected to dominate 24/7." His questioning look was met with a regretful sigh. "For too long I didn't realise that Doms can safe out too, so I played when I shouldn't have, when I wasn't in the right headspace. And because my sub needed me to, despite my protests."

"We should both use the traffic light system."

She made a note on her pad. "Thank you."

Instinctively he reached out to hold her hand. "No need to thank me; just standard respect that goes both ways. I'll also tap out, like I did just now, if I can't speak."

"Does that happen often?" she caught the glint in his eye and laughed, "Obviously for *those* situations, but I meant, do you go non-verbal as part of play very often?"

"Sometimes when I'm overwhelmed. It's not a bad thing – I quite enjoy it – but it does call for-"

"-something other than a safeword. Yes, that makes sense." She scribbled again and then looked up and grinned. "Okay, how about the fun stuff?"

His hands trembled a little as he lifted his glass, and said quickly – before she could protest, "Please can you go first?"

The look she gave him was long and searching. "Ah, a people pleaser, huh? I'd prefer it if you could tell me some first, so that I know that you're not just agreeing with what I want, to make me happy."

"I wouldn't do that!" His voice was sharp for the first time, and she looked pleased at his outburst. "This is about being honest with each other!"

She inclined her head and he sighed.

"Okay, fine. I like to serve, and I like to bring pleasure. Directed is preferable. I like not having to think. I'd like..." he stumbled over his words here, "I'd like to have someone to call Miss, to show her how much I care for her and want to please her."

Pink stained her cheeks and she breathed out her words, "Oh, you are just the most precious thing."

"How about your pet names?"

Now that discombobulated *everything*. He didn't know where to look, the floor, the ceiling, his drink, her.

Laughing, she said, "Would you like me to suggest some for you?"

He nodded, still not looking at her.

"Okay then. I'm assuming affectionate names?"

A nod.

"Sweetheart?"

Another nod.

"Good boy?"

That had him almost knocking over his drink, and fixing his gaze on her face.

"Oh." The exhale she gave was soft and pleased. "You like good boy."

He nodded vigorously.

"Does that mean that you like...you like puppy play?"

He opened and closed his mouth, goldfish-like, and just stared at her.

"It's okay, you know. Have you done that before?"

He shook his head and then let out a sigh, allowing himself to slump a little in relief. He'd always wanted to do it before, because puppy play meant bounding around, and pets and head strokes and praise, and licking. He'd get to lick enthusiastically and he was totally into the idea of that.

"W-what about you?" his words stuttered out and her reassuring smile set his mind at ease.

"I've dabbled a little with petplay before, but I've never had a puppyboy of my own. Is that something you'd like?"

"I've never been collared," he blurted out, almost ashamed of that fact. "I wanted it so so much, and I am a good sub, I promise, but I was told that I didn't deserve a collar." It had been all he'd wanted, proof that his love and devotion was enough, but it wasn't. It hadn't been. And that had almost broken him.

She slipped out of her side of the booth, "May I?"

He nodded and scooted over as she slid in next to him.

"I'm not going to say that I'm going to collar you now, because that would be irresponsible. We both need to spend some time together, get to know each other better. But I want to do that, I want to explore this with you. And besides," and here her hand raised to cup the side of his face, "I think you'd look perfect with a collar around your neck."

He felt tears prick and he shook his head, trying to pull himself together, until her hand on his arm stopped him.

"It's okay; good boys can cry too."

As tears dampened his cheeks silently, he leaned forward, needing, *wanting*, to kiss her. And he stopped, so proud of his self-control, pausing just a hair's breadth from her lips. "Please may I...?"

"Please what?"

It was that moment when each piece suddenly slotted together and he finally got to see the whole picture. He realised that this was it. He'd found her. "Please, Miss, please may I kiss you?"

"Of course." And she kissed him and everything was alright.

CATCHING ON

*S*he reorganised the cushions on the floor. Again.

She really didn't know why it was that she was so nervous; it was film night with her best friend, just like they'd done every first Friday of the month for as long as she could remember.

At first, it had been a family thing, the two neighbouring families coming together to give the parents a bit of a break, and their five-year-old selves someone else to hang out with, but even long after attendance was mandatory, the two of them had continued the tradition: in their teenage bedrooms, with buttery popcorn and posters adorning the walls; streaming on opposite sides of the country whilst at uni, FaceTiming the entire duration; and now, alternating between each other's flats.

And movie night wasn't a serious affair; art-house movies were banned. It was solely reserved for films that were so ridiculous they'd cry laughing, or ones where the number of explosions made up for a distinct lack of plot.

The last couple of months though, they'd decided to go all in on the whole pillow fort thing. Stressful new jobs, crappy exes rearing their ugly heads, and she'd made the executive decision that movie nights should be a cosy and comfortable as possible.

It had almost become a game between the two of them, trying to one-up each other on how elaborate they could make the viewing area.

She thought she'd probably won this time though.

She'd moved her sofa out of the way, purloining all its cushions to make a comfy base and back for them to curl up on. Then there were the blankets, piles of soft, fluffy wonders that they could hide under, and then she'd managed to find the largest undersheet to ever grace a bed, and turned it into a kind of canopy, attached to the bookcases either side of the tv, and floating down to rest just above where their heads would be when they sat.

And she'd fairylighted the fuck out of the whole thing.

Magical.

Even the film she'd chosen, *Mamma Mia*, was a film night classic, guaranteed to have them in fits of laughter, particularly when Pierce Brosnan sang SOS. The poor man looked veritably constipated. Brilliant.

Looking at the time on her phone, she raised an eyebrow. Running late, as ever. It was bang on when film night was supposed to start, so popping the oven on for pizzas now meant they'd be ready by the time they popped the film on.

The kitchen itself was clean and tidy. Her ADHD meant that usually she struggled with executive disfunction, and any other time of the month there'd be laundry everywhere, and dirty plates piled up in the sink, as she chose which task she'd adult and tackle that day. But on this day each month? On this day everything was spotless, almost as if she'd been body doubling with someone. Because, no matter how long the two of them had been friends, they really couldn't be more different.

She was an agent of chaos; flitting from idea to idea, free-lance consulting on so many projects at once – and all to the impressively high standard that she held herself to – so that she didn't get bored with any one individual project. Her best friend, on the other hand, well, she was all quiet focus, with impressive self-discipline, and a genuinely horror of a chaotic living room or kitchen.

So, just for her, she made sure it was all neat and tidy when she came round.

She'd do anything for her best friend.

The pizzas had been in the oven ten minutes by the time the doorbell rang, and she practically skipped over to open it.

"Hey!" She pulled the reheaded woman into her arms and hugged hard. "What d'you bring with you?"

Her friend rolled her eyes. "Nice to see you have your priorities straight, as ever. Yes I brought snacks, and yes I grabbed a bottle of wine."

She almost bounced on the spot; damn she smelt good, all coconut shampoo and *herness*. Delicious. And snacks. Snacks! "What snacks did you bring?"

There was a soft laugh as the redhead took the bag she was carrying with her into the living room, "Crisps, salty and sweet popcorn, some chocolate pretzels and oh-" Her voice cut off as she took in the sight in front of her. "Oh wow. This is...this is so *perfect*."

Her approval made the brunette flush with pleasure. "You like it? There're fairylights and cushions and blankets and even..." she got down on all fours and wriggled into the fort to grab two objects in the far corner, "...Ducks and Goose."

A gurgle of laughter met the two stuffed toys as she brought them out, offering them up on her knees for inspection. Ducks had been her own beloved comfort as a child, and Goose had been her best friend's. Many a film night had been spent under a duvet, clutching those two, even if they'd kind of grown out of them as they'd grown up.

Only when they'd realised that they were going to universities hours apart, it had hit her that she'd actually be on her own for the first time ever. She'd held her tears for the privacy of her own bedroom, but the day she'd packed up, she'd found Goose tucked into a bag with a note. *To keep you company.*

No-one would ever know what a comfort Goose had been to her, on those nights when she'd felt so very very alone. And both Goose and Ducks became her travelling companions, with her giving them their very own photoshoots wherever she went: atop fences on country walks; chilling on hotel room beds; and once, even smuggled into a super fancy restaurant.

Her best friend had made a photo album the previous year, filled with photos of the two stuffed animals over the years.

"It didn't seem right to go full pillow fort without them!"

"Definitely not!" The redhead's hand moved for a moment, as if to reach out and touch her, and she found her breath catching in her throat. But then it was back resting by her best friend's side, and her breath let out again.

"I did good?"

"You did *amazing*. Good girl." The words had a forced casualness to them, but when their eyes met, there was something else there, something unspoken that had been unspoken for a good many years now.

She wasn't sure if she wanted to leave it unspoken. In fact, she thought that perhaps one, or indeed both of them, said something, then the unspoken thing could become something rather deliciously spoken. Maybe she should-

Brrrrrrrrrrrrring.

Damn pizzas.

Scrambling to her feet, she darted into the kitchen. "Pizzas coming up."

She could feel her best friend behind her, silently watching as she flitted from cupboard to cupboard, grabbing and then discarding tea towels before she located the oven gloves and pulled those cheese-y, tomato-y delights out of the oven.

"Hey."

"Yeah?" She forced cheerfulness into her voice.

"Stop for a minute, please."

It wasn't just her who stopped, but the whole world. Time frozen for a split second and she processed every possible outcome. Every possible joy. Every possible catastrophe.

"Please, stop."

Hands took the pizzas from hers, and placed them on the side.

"They'll get cool."

"You love cold pizza."

That was true, she really did love cold pizza. But now the unspoken looked like it might be spoken and she found that she was scared. Scared of them both fucking everything up and her ending up all on her own again. She didn't want that.

Slowly, very slowly, she lifted her head, swallowed a couple of times, and met her best friend's eyes.

Her eyes were the softest grey, like the grey of Goose's downy tufts, and not for the first time, she wondered whether her best friend saw the green of Ducks' head in her own eyes.

"You've done amazingly this evening; everything looks wonderful."

She tried to fight the traitorous blush that she knew painted her cheeks, but to no avail. "Well, it's film night and…"

"I hadn't finished."

Oh. She felt heat whoosh even quicker into her face and shut up. Quickly.

"I need to tell you something, although I think you already know."

Her body lurched forward awkwardly and she found herself instinctively moving to nudge the redhead's nose with her own in the gentle way they sometimes did. Only this time it seemed oddly too intimate and she stopped, a hair breadth's away, so close that she could count each individual eyelash that framed those grey cloudy eyes. "I love you." She blurted the words out before her best friend could, so that if anyone was going to be rejected, to be hurt, it would be her. She knew how much it must have taken the redhead to make herself so vulnerable, and it was too much for her heart to handle. "Not just as a friend, though obviously, yes, as a friend too, but mainly as in I *love* love you. All hearts and shit."

"All hearts and shit." The huffed out laugh was one of near exasperation. "Come here." A hand snaked up into her hair and tugged her closer until their lips were as close to touching as their noses. "I'm going to kiss you now. If you'd like."

If she'd like? Fuck yes she'd like. She smelt the coconut of her shampoo again, but this time the scent almost drugged her. She wanted to bury her nose in those flowing flames and breathe deeply until it lived inside her, leaving an indelible impression that would never fade.

"Well?"

"Oh yes please. Kisses. Now."

That throaty laugh and then lips were touching hers and she thought she'd burst from just the overwhelmingness of it all. Lips, soft and pillowy, teasing hers; them slotting together so her chin kissed that cleft just below her best friend's lips; and the warmth, from her fingers to her toes and with all of *that* in between. Tits and the pressure of her soft belly against her best friend's and the thigh that seemed to naturally nudge her legs apart ever so slightly.

Then there was a nip and she made a noise, a kind of half squeal, half moan *desperate* kind of thing that made her so very very aware of how wet she was.

Her best friend broke the kiss, and leaned her forehead against her own, her breath jagged. "Fuck, you're just so, so *adorably needy.*"

She blinked rapidly. "Of course I am. I've needed you for so long."

That broke whatever restraint her best friend had, she found herself being grabbed by the hand and frogmarched into the living room.

"Pillow fort. Now."

Oh. Okay. She'd hoped for more kissing, but if they were doing the film first-

"Not to watch the film you twit!" Her best friend laughed and dragged her lips over hers in a lingering kiss that she felt all the way down in her cunt. "I want to see you by fairylight. If you-"

"Yes. Yes. Yes." She started pulling at the buttons of her top, frustrated when her fingers fumbled and why the fuck couldn't she just undo these damn things. Fucking buttons. Designed to prevent horny best friends from hornying all over each other.

She thumped down onto her arse and crawled into the pillow fort, her best friend following her before putting a hand out to halt her battle with the buttons.

"One second, let's not rush this."

Rush this? She'd been in love with this woman since they were twelve years old. But also, she'd been in love with this woman since they were twelve years old. Not rushing in and not fucking it up had to be at the top of the agenda. "Yeah. Good call. Ground rules?"

"Ground rules," the redhead paused for a moment. "Well, we kind of already know what each of us likes, right?"

That was certainly true. They'd shared an awful lot of sex stories over the years. "Yeah, shall we do a top three?"

"Top three?"

"Our favourite, top three, sex-related things to do."

"How about we just say what we'd like to do with each other?"

That had her attention. She wriggled, the heel of her foot tucked into the apex between her thighs, and then rocked back and forth on it a bit. "I'd like to you to tell me what to do to please you."

"Oh sweetheart, I'm definitely doing that. I want to tell you how to touch yourself for me."

Fuck. That sounded hot. "Blindfolds. I'd like to be blind-folded please."

Her best friend reached out and took her hand. "I want to sit on your face whilst you're blindfolded."

She swallowed. Yeah, that was even hotter. The idea of having one of her senses taken away so all that overwhelm could take a backseat for once whilst she fully focused on... Yup. Yes please. "And," her voice went quiet for this one, a little nervous, looking down, to the side, anywhere but at the redhead in front of her.. "And I liked it when you called me a good girl."

A hand took her chin and firmly turned it to face her. "But you *are* a good girl. And more than that, you're *my* good girl."

The breath that left her mouth was one of relief. Relief in not being rejected, but also relief in knowing that this was okay, this was alright. She was her good girl.

Her best friend knelt upwards on the cushion and then

came towards her, gently nudging her until she lay back amongst the cushions and the blankets, looking up at fairy-lights and the makeshift canopy, and her. "You were having a little trouble with your buttons there."

She resisted the urge to mutter something about fucking buttons as hands that had held hers so many times, reached out to undo the damned things.

With the release of each one, a little more of her skin was bared until her whole top was undone, almost as much as she was. Small nipples atop small breasts pebbled as the cool air touched them, and she moved her hands to smooth over the swell of her stomach and undo the zipper of her skirt.

Her stomach was the first place that her best friend kissed, red hair spilling over her skin like the fabric of a skirt pooling on the floor. The swell of it meant that she couldn't really see all the way down between her legs, but she didn't care because her own softness brought her comfort and warmth, and it seemed like her best friend liked it too.

As she kissed her way across the swathe of skin, the redhead moved her hands to tweak her bared nipples, once, twice, and then harder a third time. That felt good and she let the other woman know it, not holding back a single sound that spilled from her lips.

Usually she felt embarrassed about the sounds she made, moans and sighs and this little keening noise of desperation, but not now. Not with her. She could be wholly herself here.

Then her best friend was leaning back to pull her dress up and over until she knelt there in nothing but a cheerfully red bra and polka dot knickers. "If I'd known," she looked momentarily embarrassed, "I'd have picked out something a bit more sexy."

"Are you kidding?!" She sat up in indignation. "You couldn't be more sexy if you tried, because it's *you*, not the underwear, that makes it sexy. She leaned forward and was the one kisser this time, though that soon became kissee as her best friend turned the tables, and pushed her back once more, gathering brown hair in her fist and tugging softly.

"I'm not sure what I want to see first," the redhead whispered, running her hand across her cheek, "You blindfolded, playing with yourself, or you blindfolded, eating me out."

"Can't it be both?" because she felt needy, wanting it all right here and now thank you very much. There'd been so many years, so much time wasted, when they could have been doing this.

"Greedy girl," but the tone was gently teasing, and there was an absence of heat, whilst her best friend leaned out of the pillow fort to grab something.

The scarf she came back with had colour after colour, melting into the other, just like she felt like she was melting in her best friend's arms. "Safeword?"

"I hadn't thought of that. Traffic lights?"

"Traffic lights it is. And what about when you can't speak because your mouth is too busy licking up every drop of my desire for you?"

Her brain almost shorted out for a second at the thought of that, but she physically shook her head, and reconcentrated. "Ummmm…I'll tap out on your leg?"

"Good girl."

The words warmed her in ways that she'd never quite felt before and as the scarf was tied around her head and the world fell dark, she felt tears of relief pricking at her eyes. It was exhausting sometimes, taking everything in at such speed that she barely had time to register it all before it became another item on her list of things to sort. So having that taken away, focusing everything on sound and touch and smell and fuuuuuuuuck. Taste.

And taste was the first thing on her mind as her best

friend moved until she could sense her hovering just above her mouth.

"Are you comfortable?"

She nodded vigorously.

"Use your words baby girl, come on."

"Yes, yes I'm comfortable."

"Good." There was some shuffling around and then something smooth and hard tapped the mound above her pussy lips. "I know that trying to do too many things at once can shatter your focus, sohow about I slip this between your legs, and you can rock your needy little clit against it whilst you eat me out?"

"Oh yes please."

"Good girl, hips up."

There was an awkward moment whilst they tried to get her knickers down her legs, before her best friend gave a grunt of frustration and just ripped the gusset in two.

"I'll buy you new ones, I promise."

She didn't care. She'd rip out the gussets of all of her knickers if it meant that she got to taste her best friend.

Arching her head forward a little, she tried for where she thought it was.

"Hungry?"

"*Please.*" She'd never sounded so desperate.

Then the smooth hard thing was on her clit, rubbing against her pussy lips, and her best friend sat on her face.

It was *heaven.*

She could have lain there for hours, tasting that nectar that was so unique, so her. She alternated between delicate licks, dragging the flat of her tongue up and over, and even round, the only button she ever liked, and then taking it in her mouth and sucking hard until her best friend made a kind of squeak that let her know she was on the right track.

Completely overwhelming, and not in the ADHD, too

much input information to process kind of why, but in the fact that it was all she could think of.

No lights to distract her, just everything was taken up by the taste and smell and touch of her. By the sounds that she'd made happen. The softness of her thighs either side of her face and damn if she didn't want to stay here forever.

The thighs about her face clenched, and damn if she wasn't going to make her best friend come. She snuck an arm up and slipped her hand so that she could hold onto the redhead's hips, to give her purchase as she ground down against her tongue, and began to ride her mouth with gusto.

"Oh my good girl, my good sweet girl, you're going to make me, you're going to make me...oh." The last 'oh' was so quiet she almost missed it, but she couldn't have missed the wetness that flooded her mouth. Delicious desire, painting her lips.

She missed the feel of her best friend, imprinting upon her face, when she lifted up, but she didn't move to take off the scarf, just lay there breathing heavily, and rocking back and forth against the hand cylinder between her legs, only then that was gone too, and her hand was lifted and placed atop her lips.

"Please, darling, show me how you get yourself off."

She started then, breathing heavily as she coated her fingers with her wetness , and ran her hand between her lips and then up to circle her clit with an intensity that was spurred by the scent of her best friend, still on her lips.

It was hot, it was amazing, but she wanted, she needed...

Pausing for a moment, she tapped her fingers against whatever part of her best friend she could find, her arm, she thought.

"Yes, sweet girl? Do you need to stop?"

"I...please can I look at you?"

The scarf was loosened and then there she was above her,

grey eyes smiling kindly. "There you go; of course you can. Good girl for asking."

She felt herself glow at that, and then started again, until she was practically humping her hand whilst her best friend watched intently and stroked her hair. But it wasn't until the redhead flicked a finger casually against her nipple that she was pushed over the edge, arching up and calling out in a wordless cry of release.

Slumping back against the pillows, she tasted salt on her cheeks. Tears.

"Oh sweet girl." Her face was showered with kisses, and arms brought her close and tucked her up in them. "You were so so good for me. I'm so so proud of you."

She hiccupped thanks and buried her head in her best friend's shoulder, allowing all that tension of carrying her unspoken love all these years drift away.

It took her some time to quiet, and when she did, she found herself bundled up in a blanket, whilst her best friend slipped out of the pillow fort to get supplies. She returned with the cold pizza, snacks and a bottle of water – no wine in case of subdrop – and then slipped under the blanket to join her.

"Film night?"

And that was when it hit her. Nothing was going to change. She still had her best friend. They'd still throw popcorn at the screen during ridiculous movies. And she hadn't endangered their friendship. It was just that now that they'd caught on, they got to love each other in every other way possible as well.

PUTTING ON

*S*he was kind of frozen in place, the way she usually was after a fairly intense scene. Arse in the air, face-down on the bed, arms all floppy-like.

Fuuuuuuuuuuuuuuck.

She wasn't even sure she had any words left rattling round in her head. He might have actually fucked all the words out of her.

He chuckled behind her, and she felt the dip of the mattress, as He climbed up next to her. "Hey there princess."

Some incoherent noise exited her mouth. She tried not to cringe.

He smiled against her shoulder. "Of *course* I can give you cuddles," and then He was pulling her close and His arm, strong and warm, was wrapped round her.

Giving an experimental wriggle, she tried to see if she could move yet.

Nope, not yet.

Until she'd recovered, at least a little, she was stuck in this ever-so-becoming pose.

He let go of her for a moment, and she gave a little whine

of protest, and He kissed her cheek. "Wait one minute. It'll be worth it, I promise."

Then He was rolling her over onto her side, so that she could curl up even tighter and be thoroughly enveloped by Him, and grabbing the duvet cover to pull over them both. "Can't have my princess getting cold."

And then it was her favourite part of aftercare: the cuddles.

They'd deliberately given themselves plenty of time before work today, woken up early to start the day off right, so that they both could get all the aftercare they needed.

For her that was cuddles and hair strokes and a blanket and-

"Water?" He tapped the straw against her lips, so that she didn't have to sit up, and made sure that she drank until He was satisfied before putting it back down.

So yes, cuddles and hair strokes and a blanket and water and praise.

He needed the cuddles as much as she did; the reassurance that she was happy and relaxed after their scene; that she was okay, that He'd done a good job. He always did a good job, but she got that He needed to know that He had.

Whoever said that aftercare was only for subs didn't know what the hell they were talking about.

"Thank you, Sir. I feel all floaty."

"Good, I'm glad princess. I'm so proud of you. You did so well."

Satisfied that He was okay, she settled back into His arms, snuggling up close and lifting her hand so that she could hold onto His shoulder. In times like this, the last thing she wanted to do was let go. Letting go was not an option right now.

She was a clingy sub, she knew it, and she was totally okay with that. Because who wouldn't want to spend those blissed out moments, coming out of subspace and down from the highs of orgasms, curled up in someone's arms?

Sure, there were probably some people, no two kinksters were the same after all, but still... This was her happy place.

He was her happy place.

Solid and safe, his arms surrounding her, their bed a fort against the cold harsh realities of the world outside. She couldn't want for anything more. Never wanted for anything more than these moments of calm and soft, gentle connection.

And it was necessary for her.

She'd had that one experience, back when she'd been newly single, and in the midst of sub frenzy, meeting up with a potential Dom for a date and getting so caught up in it all that she allowed it to go way further than she usually would without safeing out. She'd had purple bruises for weeks, which she'd definitely consented to – even if she hadn't really been in the best headspace for playing – but then there'd been zero aftercare afterwards. That level of play should always come with aftercare, or at least a negotiated return to normal. She'd ended up subdropping for the first time at home, alone, shaking and crying and in a complete state. Thank goodness for her two best friends, who'd dropped everything to come over and wrap her in blankets and have an impromptu sleepover.

Poor little newbie sub her had been in genuine shock.

After that she'd made sure that aftercare was part of any kink negotiations, and that she made it clear that without aftercare, there'd be no play whatsoever.

When she'd met Him, they'd talked all of that out, and His assertion that not only did He like giving aftercare, He kind of needed it for Himself, set her mind at ease about any possible subdrop.

Things hadn't been too fast; no honorifics to begin with,

just gently trying out and exploring what each other liked, and what they liked together. Exploring what their dynamic *could* be. Until there dynamic just was and she got to wake up for kinky sex and cuddles before work.

She sighed, and He kissed her forehead. "That's a big sigh there, little one. Are you okay?"

She nodded enthusiastically. "Yeah, I'm good thanks, Sir. Just don't want to get up for work."

He rolled onto His side, to check His phone on the bedside table. "Well, we've given ourselves plenty of time, so how about you put on something pretty, and I'll cook you breakfast."

"Oh!" She clapped her hands in delight. "Really? Oh that would be *so* lovely; thank you!"

One lingering kiss and then He was out of bed, pulling on His dressing gown before heading downstairs.

She lay back, staring up at the ceiling for the moment. This was her life.

This was her life.

There were moments when she could scarcely believe it.

She got to have all this joy, all this love, all this kink. Damn she was lucky.

Instead of grabbing one of the pink babydolls under her bed, she picked His shirt off the back of the chair by her dressing table, and slipped it on. He'd worn it the day before and it still smelt like Him a little. Slightly sweaty, but in a musky way that her pheromones clearly approved of.

She only did up three of the buttons, leaving the bottom of His shirt loose to skim the tops of her thighs, and to give a nice eyeful of decolletage. Then she practically skipped down the stairs, squeaking as she rounded the bottom and almost tripped over.

"You okay princess?"

"Yes, Sir!"

The kitchen smelt *good*. Bacon and sausages sizzling in the oven, and He'd got out the fancy brioche bread, which He was toasting as she walked in.

"Don't you look delicious." He patted the high stool by the kitchen island, "Up you pop."

She climbed up and sat, swinging her legs cheerfully. "Can I have some juice please?"

"Of course you can, as you asked so nicely." He swung open the fridge door and hovered over the different cartons before landing on peach and mango. "Peaches for my peach."

He handed her the glass of juice with a kiss, and then turned back to check under the grill. "Won't be too long now princess. Bacon and sausage sandwich?"

Yum. Her favourite. He'd made it for her the first time she'd ever stayed over, and it had become a bit of a ritual for them. Nice sandwich to replete her strength after a particularly full-on play session. And this morning had most definitely been full on.

She smiled blissfully at the remembrance of it. The sharp sting of His hand, followed by the frenzied strokes and the teasing of her clit until He had her begging Him for her release, over and over. He liked it when she begged. He rarely denied her either; said that good girls like her deserved cummies when they asked for it so very prettily.

She liked asking. And she liked receiving. And she definitely liked it when He told her that she was a good girl. That was definitely her thing. It gave her that instantaneously thrill; the thrill of knowing that she was a good girl, that she was *His* good girl, and that she was doing alright. The perfectionist in her liked the fact that she was getting the validation she craved, and her logical side liked the fact that it allowed her to not hyperfocus on pleasing him in their day to day life.

But most of all, she liked sitting here on the high stool, swinging her legs and...

"What do you want to listen to?"

…and singing along to cheesy 80s music. "You pick," she said, because she knew exactly what He'd pick. Huey Lewis blared out from their Bluetooth speakers, and He sang into the wooden spoon whilst she danced in her seat.

Laughter was an intrinsic part of their dynamic: His attempts to make her laugh at his silliness; holding her down to tickle her until she couldn't breathe, she was laughing so hard; and just joy. She didn't need or want a strict Dom – her spankings were asked for and freely given – and there was something delicious about choosing to be submissive, as opposed to just following rules laid out for her.

She wouldn't change their dynamic for anything.

He'd been the sweetest person to date, taking her out for dinners and picnics and even karaoke, before taking her home and fucking her until she could barely whimper her pleasure anymore. Then kissing her down out of subspace and holding her in His arms and stroking her hair until she found herself falling far faster than she'd have liked.

The day He collared her, had been one such sweet memory, partly because the day had been about all of her, not just her subby side. Food and movies and a quiet day in, just the two of them, and He refused to fuck her, not even so much as a cheeky teasing finger, until He'd had a chance to ask her. Afterwards He'd said that it was because He didn't want her to make the decision clouded by lust and subspace, but she thought that the prospect of making love to His newly collared sub had had something to do with it also.

They'd been inseparable ever since, barely spending more than two nights apart in a row before they'd decided to look for a place together.

And now they had their little home; small but cosy, with an all-important kitchen for impromptu picnics and after-care like this, filled with knick-knacks that made them laugh:

the Dalek snowglobe on the kitchen windowsill; photos of them goofing around on the fridge; and the tiny little altar in the corner which He had accepted without even the slightest hint of amusement.

Steam released from the oven as He took the bacon and sausages out, and started constructing the most delicious of sandwiches for her. Toasted brioche bread, buttered of course, with one two three *four* slices of crispy bacon, and three halved sausages laid atop them. Then a good dollop of ketchup before cutting it in half, and sliding it across the island to her.

"A sandwich for my princess."

"Thank you, Sir!" She beamed at Him, and dove straight in, the crispness of the bacon melting into the buttered bread. A bite of heaven.

Food wasn't the be all and end all, she knew that, but she'd fast learnt that it was one of His love languages, and she was hardly about to complain. He loved to cook and she loved to eat, and so they'd ended up being practically perfect for each other.

Especially when he gave her mouthgasms like this. This sandwich was immense.

She looked up to see Him watching her. "What, Sir?"

He huffed a little smile. "Just that you're so adorable, and that I don't know how I got so lucky."

She put down her sandwich for a moment – true love indeed – and balanced on the footrest of her stool to stand up and press a kiss against His cheek. "We both got lucky. Love you."

"I love you too." He slipped round the island, abandoning His own sandwich, to kiss her. Long and sweet and tender. Taking the lapels of the shirt she wore, He pulled her close again, almost as soon as their lips parted. "My princess."

Then it was back to sandwiches and breakfast and

dancing to 80s classics before the alarm on His phone nudged them into action, grabbing final bites of food and then him jumping in the shower first, because she liked to take her time a little.

When he emerged, dripping wet, only a towel slung low on his hips, she had to avert her eyes and run into the bathroom before they got distracted all over again. Such distractions were delicious, but she could only take so much temptation before giving in and jumping him, and they both had work to do. Still, she stole a kiss and giggled when he squeezed her bum, pulling her flush against the swell of his stomach.

After disentangling herself, and closing the bathroom door firmly, so as not to be disturbed, she got into the shower and immersed herself under the stream of water. She smiled to herself. She liked that they didn't really have to rush that post-coital time; that they usually planned it so that they had the time to look after each other properly. Spontaneity was delightful in its own way, but a proper scene deserved planning, so that both of their post-scene needs could be met – especially if they were both going to make their work meetings after.

She lathered up her hair, and then let out a long sigh as she let the suds wash over her body, the soapy water caressing her skin where His hands had been only an hour earlier. It really was the best way to start her day. She felt revitalised, the way she always did after playing, and loved, and felt like she was floating on a cloud. Nothing could spoil her mood.

Turning off the water, and grabbing a towel, she got out the shower and headed back upstairs. He was already almost dressed, but he'd laid out an outfit for her on the bed.

"I know I don't do this very often, but you looked so delectable in my shirt…" A skirt, a strap top – with a bra, of course, a bust her size couldn't go without if she wanted to avoid backpain – and one of his work shirts on top. "It'll be okay for your work calls?"

"Of course; I'll make it work." It wasn't as if He'd given her an outfit that wasn't formal; she could easily femme the shirt with some accessories, though she found herself wanting to borrow one of his ties and then bounce around the house in it, asking to be tied up, instead of talking about budgets on a video call for two hours. "Thank you, Sir."

"You're welcome princess." He pulled her towards him, unravelling her from the bath sheet she'd tucked round her. "A kiss for your Sir before I have to work?"

He didn't need to ask, but she liked that He did, that He always gave her the opportunity to be happily, enthusiastically His.

And then she was drying her hair, and getting dressed, and putting on her work self for the meeting, but wearing his shirt felt like a special kind of aftercare throughout the rest of the day. A secret hug that carried him with her. Bliss.

PLAYING ON: A HITTING ON EPILOGUE

*H*e was so excited, he could barely contain himself.

They'd been together for a number of months now, played, dated and slept together – and done a lot of not sleeping too – but this was the first time that they were going to play like *this*.

He fingered the new weight around his throat, a leather band with a gold tag hanging from the front.

His collar.

It had been her gift to him the night before, an offering that had brought a shyness to his Miss' eyes that he hadn't seen since the first time she'd suggested hanging out, outside of the library. She'd told him he was a good boy, and patted his head and then had tapped out.

That had been scary; she'd never tapped out before. But he'd pulled himself up out of subspace and moved to sit next to her on the sofa, instead of on a cushion at her feet, and took both of her hands in his. "Are you okay?" His words were earnest, and they'd made her smile, which had been a relief, because he'd immediately assumed the worst.

"Oh my good boy, I'm so sorry." She'd cupped his face with her hand. "I didn't mean to startle you, but I have something serious to talk about, and I'd rather you weren't in subspace for it."

He'd thought and nodded his head. "Okay, that makes sense. What's up? Anything I can help with?"

And then she'd taken the most adorable little inbreath, as if gearing herself up, and the torrent of words that followed waterfalled down around them both. "So I love you and I know you love me, what with us having said that to each other already and everything, and we're exclusive, which I'm glad about, and our play is fantastic and you're the best sub a girl could ever ask for and so I really want to know whether you'd like to be mine?"

His face had creased in confusion. "But I am yours."

She'd blinked rapidly, and squished his cheek impetuously. "You really are the most perfect-yes, yes you are mine already. But I'd like to formalise that." And then she'd reached behind her and pulled out two boxes.

His eyes had flickered between them, torn as to which one he wanted to open first, but she made the choice for him, opening both at once.

Each box had held a collar.

The one of the left was delicate, a single band of woven leather that looked like a normal necklace might do, and the one on the right, the one on the right was an actual dog collar, with 'puppyboy' inscribed on the tag.

"They're yours, if you'll have them. If you'll have *me*." The uncertainty in her eyes was so strong that he practically dove towards her, showering her face with kisses to try and take that look away. "Yes please, *please* Miss." Her laugh made his heart sing. "You're really serious? You want to collar me?"

She moved his face back from hers firmly, and ran her hand down until it sat atop his throat, just above his Adam's apple. "Puppyboy, I've wanted to collar you from the day I met you. We just needed time to make sure that we were a good fit for each other." She leaned in until her hair brushed his cheek and he could feel her breath hot against his ear. "And we fit together very well indeed."

The collar he wore now was his play collar, his puppy collar. The other, a day collar for work and the public sphere, he wore most of the time, but she'd asked him to put this on for her after work, and wait patiently until she was done with her studies.

So he was knelt, naked but for the leather around his neck, waiting for her.

The door to her office opened, and he yipped impatiently.

"Shhh."

He obeyed immediately, raising his head to take in smart, heeled boots that ran up to her knees, and then to where bare thighs hid beneath a blue skirt, with a hemline that flirted round her legs. His cock twitched and he wanted to dive in there, but she wanted his attention; he could tell from the way she tapped her foot, and so he looked up eagerly to where she stood, smiling down at him.

"My good boy, waiting for me so patiently. Would you like a reward?"

He whined his acquiescence and then almost swallowed his own tongue in his excitement as she took out a lead from behind her back and clipped it onto his collar.

"Heel."

They'd done puppy play before, he was her puppyboy after all, but it had been less formal, and he'd never had a *lead*. He wanted to bound up and down the hallway in excitement, but instead trotted along behind her on his hands and knees into the bedroom.

That door had been closed when he'd arrived, so he'd gotten undressed in the living room, not wanting to open a door that Miss had closed, but now she opened it and tugged at his leash. "Come on, come see what treats I've got for my good little puppy boy…"

On the bed there were two parcels. He came to a stop and knelt at her feet as she sat down on the bed and looked at him. "Well, a proper puppyboy needs a proper puppy ears, and a puppy tail, don't you think?"

If he'd had a tail, he would have thumped it in agreement, but instead he nodded and licked the inside of her thigh.

Her resulting gurgle of laughter made him smug.

They'd talked about upping the puppy play, of course, she wouldn't have sprung this on him without any negotiations, but he hadn't been expecting it today, on top of the collaring the night before. He was so freaking lucky.

The ears were first, white with beige insides, on a silver headband that she slipped onto his head. He shook his head once, twice, and then pawed at them in delight. The tightness of the band on his head was not so tight as to be uncomfortable, but tight enough that he was aware of it. Aware of them, ears perked up, like a good attentive dog.

And then the tail.

He didn't know where she'd managed to find it but it was *beautiful*, the burnished brown contrasting with the white, and the detachable plug at its base.

They'd explored anal play together, and he'd found that he enjoyed taking a plug for Miss, though it was a rather intense experience, so he wasn't surprised when she patted his head, fondling the new ears for a moment, before saying "Present please."

He blushed, momentarily shy, and then turned around on all fours, and presented his arse to her.

She caressed it for a moment, delivering two gentle spanks, before he heard the lid of the lube open behind him.

That's when he started wiggling in anticipation, ready to

be filled and to wag an actual tail for her. He was so excited, she couldn't get him to stay still long enough for her to apply the lube.

"Red?"

Oh, she wanted to check in. He remained silent.

"Yellow?"

Still silence.

"Green?"

She'd barely got the word out before he started barking joyously, no embarrassment whatsoever.

"Okay okay, so we're at green, but then you need to *stop wriggling* puppyboy, or I won't be able to put your tail in."

That calmed him down, for sure. A little whimper when the cool slick gel met his skin. Her fingers danced across the opening of his arse at first, then delved deeper, stroking and widening until she had two fingers knuckle-deep in his arse. He clenched. When she stroked, just there, he felt it in the tightening of his balls and the hardening of his cock, and all the way down in the very balls of his feet.

"Good boy. Are you ready? Two woofs for yes, one woof for no."

He woofed twice, and felt himself harden, hearing the whining timbre of the sound. He sounded so desperate, so needy. So hers.

He didn't get to plead when he was puppyboy, not with words at least, but she'd come to understand each whimper and whine and cautious woof that he made; his perfect Miss.

A sharp inbreath as she pressed the cold metal up against his hole, and then working it in gently until *pop* it slid the rest of the way in, and he could feel its flared base against his arse.

But more than that was the whisper of faux fur against his arsecheeks as he moved, adjusting to the fullness. Ooooo…he moaned then, unable to hold the sound back. He had a tail. *He had a tail.*

He wriggled his bum from side to side and it moved, he could feel it move!

It took every ounce of self-control not to palm his cock then and there and stroke himself. It felt so *good*. So damn subby.

He heard her hand run across the fur of the tail and he moaned again, and then her fingers were tracing a trail up his back until they nestled in his hair again, occasionally tugging at his puppy ears.

"*Oh.*"

He could hear the sheer delight in her voice.

"Woof!"

Then there was a tug on his leash – his leash! he'd almost forgotten the collar about his neck in the excitement of it all – and he was turning round to kneel before her, tail swinging behind him as he went.

"My good *good* boy. Such a good puppyboy for your Miss."

He nodded his head enthusiastically and then pawed at her skirt, whining as he tried to nose beneath the hem.

"Oh would my good boy like something to lick?" She parted her legs and he realised, beneath her skirt, she was completely bare. No knickers, no lace, nothing between his tongue and her pussy but air.

And then she was urging his head forward, pushing him under her skirt until he was completed enveloped by the essence of her, that sweetly salty tang of her taste against his lips, and he got to lick her. He loved tasting her, and if he weren't in puppy mode, he probably would have taken his time, but he was puppyboy, and puppies were enthusiastic and he nuzzled his nose up against her clit, revelling in how wet she was before extending his tongue until he could lick her from the bottom of her pussy lips, right up to that adorably pink button at the top.

She gasped above him, and then he started to really move, licking her over and over again, getting his face messy with her pleasure until he knew his cheeks would be glistening with wetness. And all the while he listened to her.

She'd said once that the carefree exuberance of his puppyboy licking was hotter than the most skilful of cunnilinguists, that his complete focus on nothing other than licking her over and over and over until she came brought her so much pleasure.

That was what he wanted, after all, to bring her pleasure. He wanted to make her come and laugh and delight in her very own puppyboy.

Her thighs tightened about his face and he grinned, never slowing down for a second. He was going to make Miss come. He was a good boy, making sure that she had a wonderful time, wearing his puppy ears and his puppy tail and he felt his balls tighten up against, suddenly heavy and he knew, he *knew* that if she came he would too. That he wasn't supposed to come without permission, but he also wanted to make her come, and he was licking and licking and fighting to hold it back so hard until she flooded his tongue wither climax and he spilled across his own thighs, without ever once having touched himself.

He stayed there, under her skirt, ashamed of making a mess, until she lifted it and looked down at him, her eyes twinkling kindly. "You did so good, puppyboy and *oh*."

He felt his mouth dry and no, *no*, he didn't want to have disappointed her, how could he have had such poor self-control. Bad puppyboy, bad-

There was a smart rap on his nose.

"I'll have none of that now puppyboy."

He whined quietly and ducked his head, worrying at his ears with his hands.

"Stop."

He stopped.

"Now, listen to me carefully," he looked up under long lashes, taking a peek at her face. She didn't *seem* disappointed. "You're a puppyboy, and puppyboys can't be expected to be neat and tidy. Look at the mess on your face," she touched where her wetness coated his lips. "The mess on the floor is just another example of a little exuberant, humpy puppy. I'm not cross."

"You're not?" His voice seemed tinny, the first words he'd spoken since he'd walked into her apartment.

"Of *course* not." She slid off the bed, onto the floor next to him, and tugged at his leash. He felt it pull against his collar and took a jagged breath in. "You are *my* puppyboy, and you couldn't ever do anything to disappoint me. You're wearing your ears and your tail, and you licked me so so good. I'm so proud of you puppyboy."

And then he was curling up into a tight little ball, his head and puppy ears in her lap, so that she could stroke his head. "Thank you Miss."

She leaned down and kissed his forehead. "Thank *you*, puppyboy mine."

LETTING ON: A SOFTEST KINKSTERS COLLECTION EXCLUSIVE

"*A*re you sure they won't be able to tell?"

He'd never seen his best friend look quite so nervous, eyes darting backwards and forwards, completely at odds with the leather ensemble that she'd poured herself into.

"I mean, you've got me here with you. On a leash."

She suddenly looked up at him and grinned, tugging on the leash and he rolled his eyes and stuck his tongue out at her when he felt the leather collar round his neck tighten. "I do, don't I?"

"Exactly. No one could possibly know."

They'd been hanging out playing old school arcade games at his a few days earlier, when she'd said that she wanted to check out the kink club in town, he'd nodded along. It made sense; places had been starting to open back up and they'd both missed going and hanging out with other kinksters.

"Only…" she'd said, and she'd had that look in her eyes – the one that she'd had the night they'd ended up climbing over their high school fence and having a picnic on the cricket pitch, before getting suspended the following day for trespassing on school property.

"Only what...?"

"Only, I really don't want to go on my own. You know what it can be like at places for single Dommes. I'd rather scope out the place first, before I start having people come up and ask me to whip them into the middle of next week."

"Yeah, that makes sense." He'd seen it for himself, that hypnotic, captivating energy she had when she was in full Domme mode, and some of their casual nights outs had ended up with her spending most of the evening batting away advances from men, women and nonbinaries alike. "I can come with if you like?"

He considered himself to be a casual sub; liked to play, liked to have fun, *loved* a good beating every now and then, but wasn't all that interested in a permanent dynamic with a Domme of his own.

"Well, I was thinking that we could go together. As in *together* together."

That had gotten his attention alright. He'd sat up swiftly, dropping his controller. "'As in *together* together'?" He'd bounced up onto his knees to face her on the sofa and gave her what she called his puppy dog look. "Is it finally happening? Are you finally giving in to the passion you feel for me?"

She'd shoved him away playfully and grinned. "You wish."

And, just for a split second, he did.

But then she was looking at him with big pleading eyes and he'd known exactly what his answer was before she'd even asked. *Of course*, he'd go with her. And *yes*, he'd wear a collar and a leash. And *yes*-wait, no! No! No leather trousers and no bare chest.

"No?"

"I can be a convincing enough sub without it," he'd assured her, and that was how he found himself on a Friday night, half naked in leather trousers and collared up, waiting to go into a kink night with his best friend. His best friend who was almost vibrating with excitement at being able to check it out. And whose leather boots and skirt drew attention to legs that went all the way up, and an arse that most definitely bounced as she walked.

Nope. None of that.

She was his best friend, and they were faking a kink dynamic, so as to protect her from being hit on. That he could do. No one was going to make his best mate feel uncomfortable whilst he was around.

Another tug on the leash and he found himself falling into step behind her.

This would be the hardest thing, he thought, because collars were nice. They had that weight to them, and when someone tugged on a play collar that he wore? It kind of made him just want to slip to the ground and start worshipping whichever cock or pussy had put him there. Only this was *her*.

He had feelings. Lots of feelings. And no idea what to do with any of them.

Following her into the club, they went up to the bar, and she bought his drink for him – a coke with a light umbrella in it because she liked opening them up and tucking them into her bun – and another for her, before they started round the room.

They'd negotiated what both of them were comfortable with before they'd left; she could slap his arse in fun, pull him around on his leash, and he was allowed to be a little bit mouthy, but not anything that stepped too far out of bratty mode – so as not to give the game away. Flirting with each other was okay – they kind of did that jokily most of the time anyway – but no other sexualised physical contact unless they both agreed. And he had to call her Miss.

They'd even come up with safewords; just in case it all got a bit too much and they need a break. Hers was Contra, and his was Q*bert, a nod to the arcade games they'd been playing when they hatched this wild plan.

Although it seemed like they were going to get away with it.

"Hey," she tugged the leash until his ear was level with her mouth and he tried very hard not to think too much about the deep lipstick that painted her lips, and how it'd look smeared on his skin. "Shall we check out some of the private rooms?"

"Yes, Miss." The words sounded strange coming out of his mouth, and they caught each other's eye as he spoke. Any other time, they'd have burst out laughing but somehow, this time, they didn't. There was *something* – a frisson? a spark? who knew – that lent weight to the honorific.

He found himself stammering a little, attempting to "I...er...I mean..."

"It's okay," she said. "If it's too much-"

A big intake of breath and then "No!"

"No?"

"No, it's not too much. Miss."

When she smiled this time those burgundy lips were a siren song, despite their silence. "Huh."

He decided not to think too hard, but just to follow her into the neighbouring room, the two of them slipping through a door, to see a small area where a couple were slowly making out.

She cleared her throat, and when the woman looked over and nodded her acquiescence, went to sit on the couch against the wall.

Hovering above her, he wasn't sure what to do, how to sit. They'd somehow missed out this part in negotiations, though how was beyond him. Leaning towards him she whispered, "You can sit down next to me; there's plenty of space."

"But if you were here with an actual sub...?" His voice trailed off and she looked thoughtfully at him.

"If I were here with *my* sub – because you are an actual sub, even if you're not mine – I'd probably make sure there was a cushion or something, so that they could sit at my feet. But we don't have to do that."

"Would you-" his voice cracked and he tried again. "Would you mind if I sat at your-I mean, on the floor?"

There was a long pause that made him wish desperately that he hadn't said anything and was just about to throw himself onto the couch next to her, and make a huge joke out of it all, when she patted the seat next to her. "Can we talk first?"

He sank into the velvety material and avoided her eyes.

"If you can't look at me, then you definitely can't sit at my feet." That had his eyes snapping straight to her face. "Right, now, you're my best friend. You make me laugh when I'm down, come and force feed me soup when I'm ill, and are always there for me; the way I'm always there for you."

He nodded. That was true enough; the two of them would do anything for the other.

"And you have to know that when I suggested this I hadn't thought that-that we..." She blinked rapidly and he wanted to push his face up close and rest his cheek against hers until she stopped being so damn nervous.

"I know that. It's not like I thought that we would either..."

She huffed a laugh and he echoed her, their voices hushed against the gentle music playing in the background, both talking quietly so as not to disturb the couple who'd been there when they entered.

"Okay, well, if we're going to try, if you'd like to-"

"I do!" His eagerness made her face light up, and there was a wickedness in her gaze as she looked at him.

"Okay. So the rules for tonight – we'll stick with the honorifics, and-" she paused. "I need a pet name for you; something that keeps this separate in case we decide we don't want to... Have you any preferences?"

He knew what other people had called him, but he didn't want to use those. It didn't quite seem right. "I'm not sure."

"Hmmmm... How about honeyboi, because you're sweet and subby?"

Honeyboi. A flush ran up the back of his neck, and his was grateful for the muted lighting, so she couldn't see how much she'd made him blush. He liked it. It was intimate and submissive without being humiliating, and could easily be shortened to just boi if he got too bratty. "Yes please."

"Good. And no touching each other tonight, honeyboi, not like *that*. We should take this somewhat slowly, to be really, completely sure."

He wanted to assert that he was really completely sure already, but she had a point. "No touching at all?"

"Well, I can touch me, and you can touch you... And I would like to be able to stroke your hair if you're sitting at my feet...?"

"Yes please!"

His enthusiasm must have been clear, because she picked up three of the cushions that were behind her, and settled them in a pile at her feet. "Well come on then honeyboi, what are you waiting for?"

He slid off the couch, and padded over on all fours to the pile of cushions, rearranging them until he was able to sit comfortably, legs crossed. He turned to look up at her and the sight took his breath away.

Knee high leather boots, with the leather hemline of her skirt flirting just above them, a sliver of skin that seemed like an expanse between them, and then raising his eyes and looking up up up until he saw where she was looking down at him fondly.

"May I lean against your knees please, Miss?"

"You most certainly can."

He found himself slipping his arms round her boots, after getting a nod of approval, so that he could hold on whilst he rest his head against her knees. Her fingers gently reached out, and stroked his head until he nuzzled up against them and she gurgled with laughter and stroked more confidently.

"Look honeyboi," with one hand, she moved his head until he was looking at the couple in the centre of the room.

He hadn't paid too much attention to them when they'd entered, being too caught up in her, but now his breath caught as he realised that they mirrored him and Miss. A male sub, leashed, kneeling up so that he could kiss his Domme, and she laughing at him, wrapping the lead round her wrist so that she could pull him up close and kiss him brutally, plundering his mouth, before letting go, and pushing him back down.

"Stay."

The sub obeyed completely, never moving an inch, frozen in position as his Domme walked over to where Miss sat on the couch. There was a low mumur of voices, and the Miss leaned down to whisper a question in his ear. "Would you like to watch?"

Wide-eyed, he looked up at her, but she shushed him, and patted his head until he settled back down.

"She says that they would quite like an audience, and I would quite like to see how watching them would affect you. What do you think? Red, yellow or green?"

"Green." The shrill sound cut through the atmosphere and both of the Dommes laughed, Miss ruffling his hair affectionately.

"Green it is then."

As the other Domme walked back to the centre of the room, she dragged a chair with her, setting it in front of her sub, and then parting her legs until he made a little begging noise, so quiet they only just heard it.

"Would you like that?" Miss' fingers never stopped moving, stroking, and he felt himself harden. "Would you like to kneel at my feet and beg to lick my cunt?"

His whine of agreement had her fingers tightening against his scalp, the sudden sharp sensation making him gasp.

"You like eating pussy then? That's just as well, because I *love* having my pussy eaten."

There was a rip from above, and he realised that she'd torn the seam of her knickers, and then soft wet sounds assaulted his ears and he didn't know whether he should keep watching the couple in front of them, or turn around and feast his eyes on Miss.

"No no," she said, leaning down to whisper in his ear. "I want you to watch, and imagine doing that to me. I want you to watch and know that I'm fingering myself, watching you be such a very good honeyboi for me."

If he'd ever been hard before in his life, it didn't compare. His cock strained against the front of his trousers, and when she wafted two fingers below his nose, it was all he could do not to lean forward and lick them.

"You really are *such* a good honeyboi. Now, sweetness, what do you see?"

He tried to refocus on the scene playing out in front of them. The sub's face was now hidden between the Domme's legs and his rasped out an answer. "He's licking her, Miss."

"Yes, he is. And do you think he likes it?"

"Of course, Miss!"

A little laugh and then a quiet moan that almost had him

clambering to his knees and begging her to let him lick her too.

"How are hard are you honeyboi?"

He swallowed. "Very hard, Miss."

"Will you let me see?"

He couldn't undo his flies fast enough, his cock practically springing into the scene, very much wanting to be a part of whatever the fuck was happening right now.

"Mmmmmm…" Her moan had precum dripping from his tip.

"Please, Miss."

"Please what?"

"Please can I…can I…?"

Her words had a tart amusement to them that made his balls tighten up underneath him. "You have to tell me what you want, honeyboi, because otherwise I can't say yes or no now, can I?"

"PleasecanItouchmyself?" The words all ran together, and she gave a hum of approval.

"Yes, I think I'd like to see that very much."

And then he was barely aware of anything other than her fingers in his hair, the lingering smell of her desire, and his hand wrapped around his cock, jerking off for her, all whilst she continued to whisper delicious, filthy things in his ear.

"My sweet, subby honeyboi, all hard for me, wanting nothing more than to bury your face in my pussy and make me scream. To worship me until my cunt clenches on your fingers, your tongue, and I wash your face with my pleasure."

Her voice was breathy now, the words staccato, and he could hear her finger herself. She sounded sodden. Drenched. Dripping wet.

He wanted her.

"Would you like to come? Or would you like me to come?"

He hadn't known it was an either or situation, but damn he wanted to hear her come, even if he didn't get to see it. "Please Miss, please come."

"Such a good, selfless honeyboi." Her fingers clenched around his hair then and he had to grab his cock at the base to stop himself spilling as she came with a long low moan.

Then load smacking sounds as he realised she must have licked herself off her own fingers – what he would have given to watch that – and then leaned forward and said in a voice that was so soft it was a ghost, "Thank you, my honeyboi."

He let go of his cock and lent back against her knees and sighed happily. He wanted to make her sound like that always. Had always, on some level, wanted to make her happy, and now he just knew a different way to do it.

She tugged at his leash until he turned on his knees to face her. "Please may I kiss you honeyboi?"

"Yes please, Miss."

And when she kissed him, he was home.

KINK IS COMPLICATED: AN ESSAY

STEFANIE SIMPSON

*K*ink is complicated. Some fictional depictions, mostly written by non-practitioners with little knowledge of its reality, might depict it as some arrogant white cis abled man enacting violence upon a doe-eyed cis woman. Unfortunately, this narrow, patriarchal definition and expectation within wider society and readers miss many beautiful truths about kink.

In real life, learning about BDSM as one embarks on this complex lifestyle is essential and unending. The wide-reaching aspects explore everything from fundamentals of consent to psychology. We require self-awareness, control, discipline, dedication, communication, and physical knowledge. The degrees of these things will always vary because the people who partake include all intersections of society. All consensual and negotiated kink is good kink from soft Dommes who bottom to twenty-four-seven servitude.

Taboo fantasies within fiction are necessary. We can explore the forbidden safely where only the reader is the participant, and the best of these are written by people who understand kink principles and frameworks. They matter.

Real-life experiences are not demonstrated as often, but for practitioners, it's our normality. To see it in fiction as a normal and healthy facet of relationships and sex is vital to undoing the media's mistruths portrayed about kink and BDSM.

This includes breaking down ableism, racism, transphobia, binary definitions and misogyny that accompany upheld expectations without and within the kink community.

One way to do that is through fiction, showing truths within erotica and romance that unbind bad practice, demonstrating the diverse reality of kink.

Disability is part of that and of particular interest to me, being both disabled and a practitioner. Part of the reality is constant negotiation and ongoing consent. This means regular check-ins, discussion of desires, changing needs, and altering necessary frameworks. Accommodations are intrinsic to kink by nature, so factoring in disability or mental health issues should be easy enough when one starts to break down internal bias and ableism.

Frameworks can be a simple paradigm for scenes, how one looks and thinks about a dynamic, self-work to get from point a to b, or consent. For example, a scene might have a time limit. What will occur and the limits of that? What is acceptable and not acceptable language, tone and physical acts? How will it end? What aftercare will be required? This is an example of good practice both in and out of fiction.

Taking consent into consideration, a disabled person's ability to consent may not be the same as an abled person's. This might be because they are mentally ill, have cognitive issues or physically have difficulty communicating, but this should not diminish the person's ability to participate. Accommodations should be negotiated. Examining the forms of how consent is discussed and given can then inform the kind of frameworks involved when engaging in play. A good way to break it down is RACK (Risk Aware Consensual Kink). Discussing all aspects of risk. Consenting to or applying limits to risk. Using exit strategies from the word 'no', safewords such as the traffic light system and physical removal from the scene.

Seeing that on-page matters as much as disabled practitioners and educators discussing it in public forums, educational materials and kink spaces. It matters because it's a reality for disabled people.

One of the most important things in this regard within my work is *Neon Hearts*. A woman, who pre-disability was a Domme, and through adjusting to an acquired disability, reclaims that part of her sexuality. It gives her agency and power, and she does it in an accessible way. Her sub could not be in a strict sadistic dynamic, and they negotiate a gentle one.

In this case, the difference between reality and fiction is that negotiation is a long and not necessarily straightforward process. It's a gradual one, sometimes emotionally fraught or difficult. However, on-page, they accommodate each other's desires and needs while consenting to everything enthusiastically. The fundamental truth is demonstrated.

Healthy kink.

Long term relationships like this can be powerfully intense. The psychological, emotional and spiritual bond deepens love, respect and affection. Having to communicate actively and be required to think about one's actions and responses to one's partner(s) is work. It's therapeutic, but not therapy, even though it can feel like it. The reward is a transcendent profundity.

Some studies suggest that BDSM relationships are among the most healthy, which resonates with me for these reasons. However, that doesn't mean there are no difficulties beyond the HEA. The reality is that's when the work begins.

When intrinsic needs and desires change that can radically alter dynamics, and if an integral part of that relationship relies on those desires, sometimes negotiation isn't enough. There has to be more beyond the kink, so it is hard for many practitioners to find someone both sexually compatible who they want a long-term relationship with beyond the dynamic. A kink identity is not a personality trait; it's a sexual or emotional need.

Life gets in the way. And framing can help kink accommodate life changes, internal and external. Going back to the example of disability, when a partner becomes disabled, everything changes in a relationship from finance to physical presence and care requirements. The power the nondisabled person has over the disabled person can lead to a dangerous situation for the newly vulnerable person. There is an inherent risk in this situation, regardless of the type of relationship it is.

Renegotiating the type of relationship the disabled and nondisabled partners have is of utmost importance to continue the relationship, prevent it from becoming abusive or losing intimacy. Kink relationships are, in part, centred on their power exchanges. We choose the framing we partake in through the conscious roles and responsibilities we take on and tying in the types of fantasies we hold in a healthy way to explore. So including these changes into evolving dynamics has to be accounted for.

The point of any relationship is to feel an emotional connection, however that manifests, and have any physical wants met. The key difference between kink and non-kink here is becoming an active participant in the relationship you choose versus the one you have and it being a deliberate choice. Kink forces those conversations to occur.

In this collection by Ali Williams, we see all the above in action. These stories are not the meet-cute and fall in love stories. These are the ongoing explorations of what kink means in a relationship. These are long term truths. Including anxiety within kink is deeply important because mental health and healing fantasies are incredibly common. Kink can soothe or exacerbate, comfort or spiral, so a familiar reality is the right partner(s) in the right scene demonstrating ongoing negotiations, trust and consent to find subspace, control, or transcendental happiness.

It is one of kink's many truths.

As I said at the start, kink is complicated. But it is also euphoric, satisfying to the heart and soul, profound, divine, difficult, wild and controlled; it is power of self. And it's worth it.

Stefanie Simpson
Swoonies Nominee

ACKNOWLEDGMENTS

This series happened by accident, a spin off from a short story in an anthology. The fact that I'm still writing them now, shows how much I love them. But there are so many people that I couldn't have done this without. People who make my life and my writing better. Pull up a chair, because it's a long list!

To Eden Bradley and Stefanie Simpson. The two of you are that special combination of exquisite talent and a true heart. It is baffling to me that a) you agreed to contribute something to this little volume and b) that I get to call you my friends. I couldn't be luckier. Thank you for all of your support and kindness.

This series would not be what it is without its beautiful covers, both for the individual stories, and for this collection. Teresa (of Wolfsparrow Covers), thank you for being so flexible with my schedule, and for creating this cover that made me cry.

To Coralie Moss, for Vellum-ing this for me! I cannot thank you enough for your generosity and your friendship.

And as for my plotting party miscreants – D Ann Williams, Rae Shawn, K.K.H., Mia Heintzelman and Karmen Lee – I've said it once and I'll say it again: reading cards with you, attempting (and failing) to plan out my month's work, and bouncing ideas off each other has made for the most rewarding of Zoom calls. May we always call each other out when necessary, and thank you for yelling at me to go to sleep whenever I attempt to stay up way past my bedtime.

An ADHD writer (or at least *this* ADHD writer) needs body doubles; other writers to sprint with so that they don't get distracted by all of the shiny procrastination. My sprinters lift me up, cheer my gains – however small – and are such a laugh! So, thank you to K. Sterling, Fortune Whelan, Amanda Cinelli, R.M. Virtues, Reese Ryan, Katee Robert, Meka James and Lisa Kessler. Thanks also go to Aleksandr Voinov, Marie Lipscomb, Renée Dahlia, Kait Gamble, Mina Waheed and J. Emery, for being writer friends that I am truly blessed with.

And special thanks to Tasha L. Harrison and the Word-makers; our community has been there for me in a way that I shall never forget, and sharing writing experiences and stories with you has changed the way I approach this business. I'm both a better writing, and a better businesswoman, for knowing you.

Every magick practitioner needs a coven, and my Whats-Coven is myself, Holly March and Sarah E. Lily, the sweetest, nerdiest witches that I know. Your friendship brings me joy.

To my beta readers: AH, Amana, Cat, Dana, Hannah, Jacqueline, Jordan, Kali, Lena, Penny, Rebecca, Scarlett, Sonia, and Vicky. You have put up with my allergy to commas, worked with tight deadlines and always been so kind. My writing is better because of you. Thank you.

Special thanks to Angelique Migliore, for bidding in the Romance for Chencia auction, and coming up with the delicious "fake relationship with voyeurism and mutual masturbation" premise for Letting On. I hope you enjoy the story!

Everyone deserves to have a bundle of joy in their life, and mine is Agata Weronika. The kindest, softest person I know, who has flailed over each of these stories from their conception.

When N finds me chuckling away at a voice note, it has invariably come from Talia Hibbert, who is as delightful as she is talented, who encourages me to wildly enthuse over everything from brunch to Christmas decorations in her inbox, and who appreciates me whether I'm in book goblin or romance cover corset mode.

Corey. I miss you, and I wish you could have seen these stories that have been so *so* influenced by your feedback, your writing and our friendship. I hope I get to write more books that you'd have enjoyed.

Oli, Abi and Beth; the three of you got me through what was one of the hardest years of my life with your laughter, understanding and support. Here's to many more years of friendship and joy.

To my family; my loud, wildly chaotic family, whose support means more to me than they will ever know. You helped me grow into the person I am today, and the kindness in my characters is reflective of the kindness you all show each other.

N. Love of my life. Laughter in my life. Lighting up my life. (yes, soppy, I know). You showed me that it is okay to be vulnerable, and this collection of stories – which is as much about vulnerability, anxiety and connection, as it is about kink – is my exploration of that. I love you.

And lastly, to you dear reader. This collection seems intensely personal because it is, emotionally echoing the anxiety I experience in my own life. But it's also soft, and kind, and I hope it's been a gentle and comforting read.

ABOUT ALI

Ali Williams' inner romance reader is never quite satisfied,
which is why she oscillates between writing romance,
editing romance, and studying it as part of her PhD.
She can be found at the foot of the South Downs in the UK,
either nerding out over local mythologies,
reading tarot cards, or making homemade pasta, according
to her Nanna's recipes.
She believes with all of her bifurious heart that writing
romance is an act of rebellion and that academia will be so
much better when studying diverse HEAs is naturally part of
the curriculum.